MIDNIGHT WHISPERS

THE BLAKE DANZIG CHRONICLES

Visit us at www.boldstrokesbooks.com

MIDNIGHT WHISPERS

THE BLAKE DANZIG CHRONICLES

by

Curtis Christopher Comer

A Division of Bold Strokes Books

2010

MIDNIGHT WHISPERS

ISBN 10: 1-60282-186-0
ISBN 13: 978-1-60282-186-6

This Trade Paperback Original Is Published By
Bold Strokes Books, Inc.
P.O. Box 249
Valley Falls, NY 12185

First Edition: October 2010

CREDITS
EDITORS: GREG HERREN AND SHELLEY THRASHER
PRODUCTION DESIGN: STACIA SEAMAN
COVER DESIGN BY SHERI (GRAPHICARTIST2020@HOTMAIL.COM)

Dedication

For my beautiful partner, Tim.

Chapter One

O h, yeah, fuck me, dude, yeah, like that, oh…"
A bead of sweat dripped from Blake Danzig's nose and onto the muscular redhead beneath him, his lean legs thrown over Blake's broad shoulders. The twenty-something dude—who only two hours earlier had been Blake's waiter at a South of Market restaurant—certainly knew how to take cock up his ass, and Blake thrust his rubbered dick in and out of the willing ass with gusto. Blake had never really been into redheads, but his partner was tall and well-built, and his pale skin was an attractive contrast to Blake's own lean, olive-skinned body.

"You like that?" Blake asked as the kid played with Blake's erect nipples. "You like that fat cock in your ass?"

"Fuck, yeah," the redheaded waiter whispered, locking eyes with Blake.

Without warning, Blake flipped the agile redhead over and onto his knees, re-inserting his cock into the tight ass.

"Oh, fuck," the redhead said. "Yeah, that's better."

Blake resumed his thrusts. The sounds of his muscular torso slapping against the redhead's ass cheeks nearly drowned out the sound of the Mission Street traffic outside the windows.

"Shit," the redhead moaned, "I'm coming."

The tug of the redhead's asshole on Blake's cock as he shot his load coaxed Blake into his own orgasm.

"Fuck. Here it comes," Blake gasped as he filled the rubber he was wearing with an ample load.

Breathing heavily, Blake collapsed onto the bed beside the sweating redhead.

"I'm sorry." The redhead laughed. "You really got me off in that position."

"That's okay." Blake smiled at him. "Did you say your name was Daryl?"

The redhead leaned over and kissed Blake lightly on the lips.

"Darren."

Blake admired Darren's pale, wiry body and muscular ass as he rose from the bed, crossed the room, and pulled on a pair of black boxer briefs.

"Sorry," Blake said. "I meet so many people, I tend to forget names."

Admit it, Blake thought. *You don't remember names because you fuck so many people.*

But Blake hadn't chosen a promiscuous life. No guy, once he learned of Blake's "gift," tended to stick around very long. All Blake really wanted was companionship, the possibility of finding the one person who might see beyond his paranormal abilities and stick around longer than one night. That was how, after checking out his waiter's ass all night—and getting busted numerous times—he had ended up in Darren's Mission Street apartment.

"So one of the busboys told me you're like a ghost hunter or something," Darren said, mild amusement on his face. "What's up with that?"

"I'd rather not talk about it." Blake rose from the bed.

"Come on. Are you? I mean, do you actually talk to ghosts?"

Blake pulled on his jeans and faced Darren. "Yeah. I'm a ghost hunter."

Darren sat on the edge of his bed and looked up at Blake, grinning. "I'll bet lots of poor suckers pay you tons of money to talk to poor old, long-lost Grandma, huh?"

Blake could feel his face reddening as he pulled his T-shirt over his head. It was always like this. Guys either freaked out over the fact Blake could talk to ghosts, or they were absolute skeptics, like Darren, who obviously believed Blake was a fraud who bilked old ladies out of their savings. Blake wanted to prove his powers, but resisted the urge to tell Darren about the ghost standing just two feet away from him. He had learned a long time ago divulging such information to the absolutely clueless was not only mean, it could be harmful.

"I'll see you around," he said, heading for the door and leaving Darren alone with the ghost in his bedroom.

Out on busy Mission Street, Blake raised his hand to hail a passing cab. Unfortunately, the cab was occupied and the couple inside, so obviously a couple, made Blake feel even more lonely. He sometimes wondered if leaving his family and the circus had been the right choice. At least with his family, he told himself, he hadn't been so alone. At least they had understood his gift.

Blake had been born into a circus family. The Danzig Brothers Circus, part circus, part carnival, had been created by Blake's great-grandfather in the 1930s and traveled the back roads of America. After the death of Blake's grandfather, Blake's father had taken over the management of the circus. Blake's mother, Lila, was the tarot card reader and his father, Ben, a contortionist. Both parents were aware of their young son's "gift" and encouraged it. By his tenth birthday Blake was made an official part of the circus and, for five dollars a pop, could contact the dead relative of any paying customer.

Halloween, however, was the worst for the young Blake. Although he learned most ghosts were harmless, Halloween was a special challenge due to the sheer number of them wandering aimlessly through the physical plane.

"On Halloween," his mother had calmly explained, "the veil between the world of the living and the world of the dead is thinnest."

Blake's mother, Lila, never explained exactly how she knew about "the veil" and he never asked, only took her word for it. Others in the troupe whispered that Lila's mother had also been able to speak to spirits. On this subject, however, Lila kept quiet, only telling him that he had inherited his gift.

As a result, Halloween became a dreaded day for Blake. Not because of any evil, but because the sheer number of ghosts whispering in his ear was too much to bear. The real trick was to avoid the people *not* in costume. The revelers dressed up as ghouls were safe, but the real ghosts looked like everyone else, only sometimes in period costume. Every night, at midnight, the whispers of the spirit world would grow loud for the young Blake, causing him to nickname the phenomenon the "midnight whispers."

Blake had loved growing up in a circus. It had certainly not been a typical childhood, the ragtag caravan constantly on the move from one small town to the next. Despite the fact he'd grown up without any other children to play with and had been schooled by his mother instead of attending a traditional school, the experience was a constant fantasy world for him. Instead of a normal home, there were spotlights and greasepaint and colorful banners. Instead of aunts and uncles, Blake had a strong man and a fat lady and a sword swallower.

Instead of a dog or a cat, Blake had an elephant for a companion. But while he loved the massive pachyderm named Moe, he often felt sorry for the poor creature. Even though he was young, Blake instinctively knew an elephant did not belong in places like Oklahoma or New Mexico or Kansas. He also knew the chain around Moe's ankle was cruel. He voiced his concerns to any adult who would listen but was always brushed aside—even by his father, who explained the chain was necessary for everyone's safety. This explanation made no sense to Blake, who found it difficult to believe the gentle giant would harm a fly. His misgivings, however, were realized one night in a small town outside of Topeka when Moe, terrified by a thunderstorm, broke free of his chains and rampaged through the small downtown before the sheriff shot him dead. It wasn't long before Blake, by this time a young man, decided it was time he needed to break free of the circus, too.

It was on his twenty-first birthday that Blake made up his mind he was finished with the circus and ghosts and announced to his parents he was moving out West. He had grown into a handsome young man, tall and muscular, with the olive-colored skin, brown eyes, and dark hair of his Latina mother. He'd decided on San Francisco.

Although his parents were disappointed, they quietly accepted his decision and wished him luck.

"It's just as well," his father said. "This can't go on forever." He waved his arm at the scenery around them. "I'll probably retire in a couple of years anyway."

Blake smiled, enjoying a private joke. Ben had been saying he intended to retire for years. Still, times had changed, and people weren't as interested in circuses as they once had been. The only circuses that would eventually survive would be the polished, corporate versions, so maybe his father had been right.

❖

Lost in thought, Blake nearly missed the next cab as it sped up Mission Street. He raised his hand just in time and the taxi screeched to the curb. Grateful to have caught it, Blake opened the back door. He slid into the seat, quickly giving his street number to the driver, a dark-haired guy in his thirties. Settling in for the short ride back to his Nob Hill apartment, Blake glanced out the window at the passing scenery. The cab driver kept looking at Blake in the rearview mirror, but if he recognized the young celebrity in his backseat, he kept quiet. Once they had pulled to a stop in front of Blake's condo, and Blake paid the fare, the driver looked at him closely.

"Hey, you're Blake Danzig, aren't you?" he asked.

Blake merely nodded.

"I'm a big fan of your show. It's really amazing, that gift of yours."

Blake thanked the driver for his kind words and wished him a good night. As he entered his building he thought about what the cab driver had said. Sure, his ability had brought him fame, but at what price? Was his gift really so amazing?

Amazing if you want to remain single your whole life, Blake thought. The cold wind that filled the night air did nothing to cheer him. He turned and walked into the lobby of his building, filled with the sad feeling of spending another night alone.

CHAPTER TWO

B lake entered his apartment and looked around at all he'd amassed in such a short time. The comfortable apartment, definitely a man's abode, was filled with new furniture in subtle shades of brown and gray. The furnishings—a sofa, coffee table, TV, bookshelf, two comfortable armchairs, and a dining room table that could accommodate eight—served only the necessities of life. On the wall above the table hung a simple, framed watercolor, purchased at an art fair. Other than that small touch, the remaining walls of Blake's condominium were bare. The two bedrooms, too, were outfitted with only the essentials—beds, nightstands, and dressers. Blake walked over to the windows and marveled at the city, spread out below. He went to the bookshelf and took down his book, *Haunted: My Life as a Carnival Medium,* the vehicle that had propelled him to fame. His thoughts turned to his past and all that had happened after he left his parents and the circus.

His parents had, of course, insisted on driving him to an Amtrak station to see him off. This meant not only that they would be with him right up to the last minute, but it would delay his departure until the circus caravan was able to swing by a city with a train station, in this case, Kansas City. Both Lila and Ben, after much difficulty doing so, had convinced him that his idea of hitchhiking to a train station was not only foolish, but dangerous.

"Besides," his father said, "there are too many loose ends to tie up before you run off to California." And so Blake had grudgingly stayed on, long enough to reach Kansas City. Once there, in the presence of Anna, aka the Fat Lady, and Simon, touted as the World's Tallest Man, Blake bade his parents a teary farewell.

Passersby in the crowded station eyed the odd-looking party with a mixture of amusement and curiosity, but Blake ignored them.

"You call as soon as you get there." Lila sniffed, not bothering to hide her tears.

Blake hugged his mother tight.

"How will I reach you?" he asked, amused by his mother's absentmindedness. Cell phones weren't yet commonplace, and the traveling circus depended on pay phones for any contact with the outside world.

"We'll be in Cedar Rapids in a week," Ben said. "Call their post office and leave word for us, with a phone number if you have one. We'll get your message."

All Blake was taking with him was five hundred dollars he'd saved from his portion of the proceeds, a duffel bag containing two pairs of blue jeans, four T-shirts, socks, and six pairs of clean underwear. He was wearing everything else. Impetuously, Lila removed the St. Christopher medal she wore around her neck on a chain.

"You take this," she said, placing it around Blake's neck. "It will keep you safe."

"Thanks, Mom," he replied, tucking the medal under his T-shirt.

Blake boarded the train and took a seat at a window near

where his family stood on the platform. As the train pulled out of the station, he returned their waves and watched as they slowly faded from sight. With each inch the train moved, each mile, Blake could feel an excitement building inside of him, an excitement for the new and uncharted. Blake did his best to quiet his doubts, the thought that maybe he was making a mistake.

The first night on the train was exhilarating. Although filled with a mixture of melancholy and fear, Blake was also filled with anticipation. Not only was he headed to San Francisco, but nobody on the train knew he could see and talk to ghosts or that he had just left a circus. For the first time in his life, he was truly on an adventure.

Blake looked around the crowded car. There were ghosts, of course, but he did his best to ignore them by refusing to make eye contact. No, ghosts were the last thing Blake wanted to deal with on the first day of his new life. He peered out the window at the passing scenery, reminded of his childhood and all the places the circus had taken him. A voice behind him jarred Blake from his thoughts.

"Is this seat taken?"

Blake turned to see a tall blond in his early twenties standing in the aisle. He motioned to the vacant seat next to Blake for clarification.

"No," Blake replied.

The blond, wearing khaki shorts and a T-shirt with the UCLA logo, placed his backpack in the overhead bin before sitting down beside Blake. The clean-shaven new arrival had a nice chiseled jawline and high cheekbones. His blue eyes twinkled when he spoke.

"I'm Chance," he said.

"I'm Blake." Blake offered his hand.

"Where are you headed?"

"San Francisco." Blake admired Chance's muscular calves and his chest, which was bulging inside his tight T-shirt.

"Great city. Are you visiting friends, or do you live there?"

"I live there. Well, I plan to live there—"

"Wow," Chance said. "You're moving there right now. How exciting."

Chance shifted in his seat and his bare leg came to rest against Blake's leg. Blake swallowed and felt an erection stirring in his jeans. He couldn't move, afraid Chance would move his leg away. He sat, silently staring at the muscular leg, mesmerized by the blond hairs covering it.

Blake had never been with another man. He had been attracted to plenty of them: visitors to the circus, clerks in shops, even a brief crush on the strong man, but had never had the opportunity to act on his urges.

When Blake finally looked up, Chance was staring at him, then asked, "Are you gay?" His voice was barely audible.

Blake felt his face flush. "Yes," he managed.

He locked eyes with Chance, astonished at how blue his eyes were. Blake wanted to say something but his mouth felt dry. He wanted to touch Chance's face but felt riveted to his seat.

A smile slowly crept across Chance's handsome face. "Come on," he said, rising from his seat. "I have a sleeper car."

❖

Sex with Chance was amazing. For the first time since leaving his parents in Kansas City, Blake felt certain he had done the right thing by leaving. No longer a virgin, he now viewed his new adventure in an entirely different way. He was no longer a child, and he felt as if he could accomplish anything. Finally, life was starting to make sense. Hungry for the physical contact he had only imagined up to that point, Blake had sex multiple times with Chance on their trip west. And Chance, though seeming astonished and physically exhausted by Blake's stamina and sexual appetite, clearly appreciated his beautiful body and desire to fuck.

"You could always move to LA instead," Chance suggested.

Blake shook his head slowly. "I've pretty much decided on San Francisco. Besides, I bought a travel guide and everything." He pulled a San Francisco travel guide from his bag. "You could stay in San Francisco."

"I live in LA," Chance said. "Besides, I have to get back to school."

Neither of them said anything else until the train was at the station.

As they parted, they promised to keep in touch. Chance wrote his phone number on a piece of paper. "Call me if you're ever in Los Angeles." Chance winked at him. "I wouldn't mind seeing you again."

"I will," Blake was sorry to part with his new friend so soon. He folded the paper and tucked it in the back pocket of his jeans.

He waved good-bye to Chance and carried his bag out onto the busy street, pausing to retrieve his San Francisco travel guide. As he did so, the paper with Chance's phone number slipped unnoticed from his pocket and drifted down the street, carried by the wind.

He was just the first of many Blake would forget.

❖

Blake had picked San Francisco as his home not just because of its tolerant attitude toward gays, but also for its bohemian atmosphere. At least in San Francisco, Blake had reasoned, the fact that he came from a circus family shouldn't seem too weird.

He took an apartment in the North Beach neighborhood, situated above an Irish pub. As promised, he called his parents with his new address and quickly found work at an Italian bakery around the corner. Although Blake had no formal training, the owner, a boisterous Italian American named Carlo, was happy to have the help and taught him everything he knew. North Beach did little to free Blake of his ability to see ghosts and was full of spirits: the ghosts of Barbary Coast bandits, Chinese immigrants, and dead Beat Poets. The spirits of Janis Joplin and gangsters roamed the streets of the lively district beside the spirits of World War Two sailors and soldiers.

Blake might have made a quiet life for himself there, except for a chance encounter one evening after work. Sitting at a sidewalk table at the Irish pub below his apartment, he had been joined by a blond woman in her fifties sitting at a neighboring table. She was tastefully dressed in a taupe, two-piece suit with matching high heels, and it was obvious that her matching bracelet, necklace, and rings had been carefully chosen. She was glamorous in a way only European women could successfully manage and was drinking a glass of red wine. She introduced herself as Donatella. As she prodded him for details of his life, Blake finally broke down and, somewhat sheepishly, admitted he'd grown up in a circus. The further confession that he could speak to the dead had made Donatella gasp. Blake sensed her skepticism.

"Prove it," she had said, and touched Blake's arm. "Show me your gift."

Blake sighed. He was in no mood for theatrics, especially at a sidewalk table. But part of him was angry at her because she didn't believe him and because, like so many others, she couldn't see what was right in front of her.

Or, in Donatella's case, right behind her.

"What do you want to know?" he had asked, and glanced from side to side to make sure no one else was listening.

"Anything," she said, her eyes sparkling. "Are there any ghosts here?"

Even though the sidewalk was alive with pedestrians and traffic was heavy on Columbus Avenue just a few feet away, she looked around as if they were alone in a darkened, haunted house.

Blake closed his eyes and inhaled deeply. When he opened them and looked at the expectant Donatella, he saw a bright, hazy light just over her left shoulder. As he stared at the light an old woman's face came into focus.

"Your Nana is here," he said, still looking at the ghost of the old woman. "She says the china was meant for you and not your little sister."

Donatella jumped up and Blake was afraid he had said too much. She reached into her Gucci handbag and produced a business card, which she passed to him, her hands shaking.

Blake took the card but, before he could look it over, Donatella stepped away from her table and out onto the sidewalk.

"Call me," she said, visibly shaken. "I think we can work together."

As she retreated down the sidewalk, her expensive shoes noisy on the concrete, Blake looked down at the embossed card in his hand.

Donatella Ferrari
Literary Agent

❖

Blake was surprised at how easy writing came to him. Under the guidance of Donatella, Blake's first book, *Haunted: My Life as a Carnival Medium*, became an instant bestseller. Suddenly, Blake was thrust into a spotlight he hadn't quite counted on. There were book signings and lectures and even an interview in a PBS piece on the existence of ghosts. Thanks to Donatella, Blake was making more money than he knew what to do with. His first large purchase was a two-bedroom condominium perched atop Nob Hill.

The prestigious address suited his new celebrity well, and from his living room windows Blake could see the Fairmont, the Mark Hopkins, and the Huntington hotels, the elder "gentlemen" of the hill. Just past the Fairmont, downtown San Francisco, Union Square, and the financial district spread across the landscape, leading up to the bay and the famous Bay Bridge. From his bedroom window Blake could see Chinatown and North Beach and, past that, Alcatraz and the distant shores of Sausalito. He felt like a king or an emperor up on the hill with its impressive views, the spectacle made all the more dramatic at sunset, when the dying sun in the west illuminated the surrounding hotels in fiery splendor.

His second expenditure—the brainchild of Donatella— was to open a business, Danzig Paranormal Investigations, in a small storefront on the edge of Chinatown. Donatella had reasoned that with the success of his book, he would surely draw customers in need of his assistance. As usual, Donatella's instincts had been right and, within a very short period of time, Blake had more business than he had imagined possible. The owners of haunted houses, apartments, and businesses kept Blake busy. Usually, Blake would merely ascertain for the owner whether the spirit was malevolent. Often, with the spirit's consent, Blake would help them "cross over," thus ridding the premises of the spirit.

Blake's next big break also arrived thanks to the machinations of the resourceful and well-connected Donatella. Gambling on the success of Blake's book, she had approached the FX network with an idea for a ghost-hunting show based, in part, on the already existing success of the genre. Unlike the competition, she had argued, Blake's gift was real and the fans of his book would become loyal viewers. Blake had at first balked at the idea of television, but when he realized he would be able to travel and that the pay was ridiculously high, he relented. Besides, Blake told himself, traveling around California would give him the opportunity to meet lots of men. The show, which aired under the title *Haunted California*, was a huge success. The premise was simple and only expanded what Blake already did in San Francisco. He would visit supposedly haunted locations—houses, museums, hotels and parks—and communicate with any spirits that resided there.

Along with a camera crew, the network paired Blake with Melody Adams, a self-professed witch and clairvoyant. Although Blake had never doubted his gift, he was grateful for the assistance Melody offered, as his own skills had nothing to do with clairvoyance or psychic work. He was a medium, period, and had always shied away from the all-encompassing terms "psychic" and "clairvoyant." Melody, however, was a clairvoyant in the true sense of the word. She could sense things in people and places in ways that amazed even Blake. Together, they made a team that the viewers of *Haunted California* came to love.

Still in his early twenties, with more money than he ever imagined, Blake had grown into quite the successful young man, with a best-selling book, a thriving business, and his own television show. And, with his unassuming good looks, he quickly began to meet men attracted to his good looks and success.

And then he met Brian.

CHAPTER THREE

B rian Cox was a detective with the San Francisco Police Department. He'd been sent by the department to check out Danzig Paranormal Investigations, with the hope the supposed "ghost talker" could help them solve a number of unsolved murders. Brian had, of course, seen *Haunted California* but was still skeptical. In his opinion, shows like Blake's were frauds. As a cop, Brian was more interested in physical evidence than smoke and mirrors.

His Irish Catholic upbringing, paired with the no-nonsense approach toward life instilled in him by his father—a retired cop—had made Brian an almost stubborn skeptic. For him, the proudest moment of his life was the day he joined the force, following in the footsteps of his father and grandfather. He was one of the first openly gay cops on the SFPD.

Blake had later told Brian that he'd been smitten with him the moment he stepped into his Chinatown storefront. Brian, too, instantly felt attracted to the tall, dark-haired "ghost talker," almost forgetting why he was there in the first place. Although he had already noted from watching the show that Blake was handsome, whereas Brian had expected to find a smarmy, argumentative guy he found instead a warm and charming human being. And television did no justice to Blake's eyes, the warmest brown Brian had ever seen, accentuated by his dark, heavy eyelashes and dark, thick brow. Blake's full lips, too, seemed to glisten when he spoke and, although Blake's attempt at a mustache and goatee were mere wisps, Brian was filled with the urge to nibble at the wiry growth sprouting from the ghost talker's chin.

Brian had planned to barge in, display his badge, and barrage Blake with questions, but his unexpected attraction left him confused and unsure where to start. After an awkward introduction and flash of his badge, he finally blurted out the reason for his visit. Blake had only taken Brian by the hand, a tender gesture that surprised him.

"I'm used to skepticism," Blake replied. "But ghosts are real. In fact, you have one that follows you everywhere."

"Really?" Brian looked nervously from side to side.

"Would you like to know who he is?"

"He?"

Blake, still holding Brian's hand, gazed just over his shoulder. Brian felt cold chills creep up his neck and quickly pulled his hand from Blake's grip.

"Prove it," he said, unnerved. "Who is he?"

Blake seemed to listen to something. "Your grandfather. He still wears his old uniform and follows you everywhere. He says he doesn't want what happened to him to happen to you."

Brian could feel the blood drain from his face, and Blake looked concerned. "Are you okay?"

"My…my grandfather was a cop," Brian stammered. "He was killed in a botched bank robbery twenty years ago…out in the Sunset District."

"He says he's very proud of you. And he loves you."

Although Brian had been only six years old when his grandfather died, he still had fond memories of the gruff old cop, and tears stung his eyes.

"Thank you," he finally managed. "I expected to come in and find a fraud, but instead you…you really blew my mind."

Blake passed Brian a tissue and, after he had wiped his eyes, Blake took his hand again. Brian dabbed his eyes, embarrassed by his sudden emotions.

"You're not married?" Blake asked.

"No." Brian laughed, feeling suddenly emboldened. "I'm gay."

Without comment, Blake rose from his seat and walked to the door. He flipped over the sign hanging on it so it read CLOSED from the outside and locked the door. When he returned, Brian was standing.

"I'm on duty," he said, weakly.

"So am I." Blake pulled him close.

His defenses gone, Brian surrendered to Blake, allowing him to loosen his tie and unbutton the top few buttons of his shirt. They kissed passionately, their hands moving over each other's bodies with a sense of urgency neither of them could deny. Brian's body tingled at the sensation of Blake's wiry upper lip pressed against his face, and he groaned loudly as Blake began to lick and suck his exposed nipples. He found the outline of Blake's erect cock through his jeans and fought with the button fly for a moment before freeing the hard-on inside. Then he dropped to his knees and greedily swallowed the throbbing erection, causing Blake to gasp loudly.

"Fuck, yeah," Blake whispered. "Swallow that fat cock."

Brian sucked hungrily on the massive boner and pulled his own erection out of the front of his slacks, slowly masturbating as he gave Blake head.

"Fuck." Blake groaned. "That taste good? You like the taste of that fat dick?"

Brian merely grunted his approval.

"You want that fat cock up your ass?" Blake teased him.

Brian looked up from his kneeling position on the floor and their eyes met. He managed to nod and released Blake's cock from his lips. "Do you have a rubber?" he asked.

Blake slowly nodded, never moving his eyes from Brian's, and pulled him to his feet. He kissed Brian on the mouth, letting his tongue explore inside, and relished the taste of his own cock on the young cop's lips. He grasped Brian's meaty dick in his hand and felt him tense at the touch. With his other hand, Blake lowered Brian's slacks and boxer shorts and reached around him, feeling his round, smooth ass. Brian inhaled sharply as Blake began to tease his asshole, touching the tight, pink ring.

"Turn around," Blake whispered.

Brian complied and Blake pushed him over the cluttered desk in front of him. Bent over the desk, with his pants around his ankles, Brian quaked in anticipation as he could hear Blake, behind him, stripping off his jeans. Brian peered to one side for a better look and was turned on to see Blake, totally naked, standing behind him. His chest and legs were a mass of curly black hairs that covered his olive skin, and his erection, thick and veiny, pointed at the ceiling. Without a word, Blake knelt behind him and spread his ass cheeks. Brian was afraid he might shoot his load when Blake stuck his tongue in his ass and began rimming him.

"Fuck," he groaned, grasping the desk beneath him. "Yeah, eat my ass."

Blake grunted and shoved his tongue in deeper, rimming the tight, willing ass in front of him. He pulled back and teasingly licked the pink anus and ran his tongue over the sparse blond hairs that encircled it. Then, without warning, he shoved his tongue back in and licked inside, savoring the flavor of man ass.

The sensation of Blake's wiry facial hair on his ass was nearly too much for Brian to bear.

"Fuck me, Blake," he groaned. "I want your dick inside me."

"You ready for it?" Blake was working a finger into Brian's asshole.

"Yes, please."

Blake arose from his position on the floor and spun Brian around. He pulled off Brian's pants and tossed them onto a nearby chair and unbuttoned the remaining buttons on his shirt. This he tossed, too, onto the chair, leaving Brian wearing only his striped tie, which was flung over his shoulder. With one hand, Blake opened a drawer on the desk and produced a condom and a bottle of lube. Brian watched as he opened the condom wrapper with his teeth and expertly rolled the rubber onto his stiff cock, then poured a bit of the lube onto it.

Now lying on his back across the desk, Brian lifted his legs as Blake pulled him closer, and he gasped loudly as Blake pushed his swollen meat into his ass.

Blake looked down and admired how beautiful their bodies looked together as his dick slid in and out of the man beneath him.

"You like that?" he asked, their eyes meeting again.

"Fuck, yes. Fuck me, Blake."

"Jesus, Brian…"

Before Blake could finish his sentence, his nuts tightened, his nipples became erect, and a dizzy feeling came over him. He unloaded into the condom for what seemed like an eternity and continued fucking until Brian shot his own load onto his tight, white torso.

Blake collapsed onto Brian and, breathing heavily and sweating, neither of them moved for a very long time.

"Well," Blake said, finally, rising on one elbow, "I think we're going to work together just fine, Detective."

CHAPTER FOUR

"Are you excited about your first case?" Brian asked. He looked from Blake to Melody, who had met him at police headquarters to begin work on some reopened cold-case files.

"Of course," Blake said. "What is it?"

"Do you remember a serial killer the press dubbed the Doodler?"

Blake nodded, but Melody shook her head. "Vaguely," Blake said, "but we were all pretty young when that happened."

"Why was he called the Doodler?" Melody asked.

"Because," Brian held open a door for his two guests, "at the scene of each murder he left graphic cartoons of the slayings. The murders all took place on or around Twin Peaks, so we believe he lived up there."

They walked through a metal detector and Brian continued talking.

"Anyway, the SFPD has long been criticized for not solving the killings, and Police Chief Norris is feeling a little heat from the families of the victims. You," he said, looking at Blake, "are his last hope."

"That's encouraging." Blake laughed.

"Chief Norris is no fan of psychics," Brian replied, his voice low. "That's why you, Melody, might not want to mention that you're a witch."

"Should I also leave out the fact that I'm a lesbian?" she asked, her eyes narrowed.

Brian ignored the comment.

As he and Melody followed Brian through the labyrinth of the central station, visitor tags affixed to their clothing, Blake couldn't help but have a little fun with his new boyfriend.

"You know, Brian," he whispered, "there are ghosts all over this place."

"I don't doubt it. But that's not why you're here." He shuddered slightly. "Besides, I *work* here…I'm not sure I want to know how many ghosts are lurking around every corner."

They walked through a door marked Evidence, and Brian passed a piece of paper to a gray-haired cop standing behind a mesh barrier. The cop looked at it, then looked back at Brian before disappearing around a corner. Five minutes later he reappeared carrying a manila folder, which he passed through a gap in the mesh just above the small counter. In turn, Brian signed a document, which he passed back to the cop.

"We ever gonna catch that bastard?" the cop asked.

Brian lied. "Looks like we're going to give it another shot, based on new evidence."

"New evidence?" The cop shook his head and walked away from the window.

Brian led Blake and Melody to a conference room just four doors down. He flipped a light switch, and the stark neon lighting and lack of windows made Blake feel slightly queasy. The room was Spartan, with nothing more than a worn conference table and six industrial-looking chairs in the center. How could Brian work in such a place day after day? For someone who had basically grown up onstage, such surroundings seemed almost claustrophobic. Still, somebody had to do this kind of work, and if it weren't for people like Brian, who would? Blake glanced around the room again with a shudder.

He and Melody took a seat on either side of the table, with Brian sitting at the end, facing them both. He opened the evidence folder, pulled out papers encased in clear plastic sleeves, and began laying them out on the table between him and Melody. Each sheet contained a crude drawing portraying violent scenes. The drawings, not much better than stick figures, were accompanied by frantic, scrawled messages. Melody picked one up and grimaced at the image, a woman with curly hair and her throat cut. The words "stuck-up bitch" were written across the bottom of the page, along with the date.

"Jesus," she muttered, picking up a drawing of an Asian woman with long, dark hair. The wounds on the Asian woman appeared more numerous and were on her arms, legs, and torso. The legend "screaming bitch" accompanied this drawing. Disgusted, Melody pushed them away, ignoring the rest on the table.

"What a psycho," she said, a pained look on her face.

Blake flipped through the drawings and nodded. Although the murders had occurred before he was born, he'd read about the Doodler—maybe in the papers, he didn't remember. Like most people, he'd wondered what had happened to the elusive killer. Most people assumed that the Doodler was dead, others speculated he had simply stopped killing for fear of getting caught, and although Blake hadn't given too much thought to it, he'd supposed the man was simply in jail, locked up for another crime.

"Did you pick anything up from them?" Blake asked Melody.

"You mean, besides the guy was a sexist asshole who had serious issues with women?" Melody asked, curling her lip.

"I could pick that up, and I'm not psychic," Blake said, "but did you get any, you know, vibrations or anything from them?"

Melody sighed loudly and picked up one of the drawings. "I'm glad these are encased in plastic. I'd hate to catch the crazies from them."

She was silent for a moment and closed her eyes. "He lived near Twin Peaks," she finally said. "He knew his victims, and his name began with a J."

"We know he lived near Twin Peaks and that he knew his victims," said someone new, startling Melody into opening her eyes. "Christ, we've had psychics tell us that since day one." He said "psychics" the way some people said a racial epithet. "And, as far as the letter J goes, that's a new one. That should narrow things down." His voice dripped sarcasm.

"Good afternoon, Chief Norris." Brian quickly rose from his seat. "We were just reviewing the evidence." He kept his voice even. "This is Blake Danzig and his friend Melody. Blake, Melody, this is Chief Norris."

The chief, a barrel-chested man in his early fifties, merely nodded at them. His gray hair was closely cropped and a triangular scar rested above his right eye. His white shirt was pit-stained and his tie was a floral print that resembled a Hawaiian shirt. He turned back to Brian, his expression serious.

"I didn't agree to any more psychics," he said, with no regard to Melody's presence. "They've been no help to us for the last twenty years. I only agreed to bring in the ghost talker here because you said he really can talk to ghosts."

"He will," Brian stammered, seeming embarrassed. "I thought this might be a good start." He shrugged. "We have to start someplace."

The chief scowled before abruptly turning and walking out.

Brian closed the door and returned to the table. "I'm sorry about that. He's not a big believer in this sort of thing."

"How does he expect me to find the ghost of one of the victims?" Blake asked. "I can't just pick up a piece of paper and talk to ghosts. It doesn't work like that, Brian."

"That's what I haven't told you. There's talk that an area up on Twin Peaks is haunted. It's the same area where they found one of the victims."

❖

The traffic on Market Street was fairly light, so the drive up to Twin Peaks was a short one. Although Blake was afraid of what they might find there, the day was crystal clear as they made their way up the twisting road to the top. Once they were there, the vista was breathtaking, with clear views of the ocean to the west and the Oakland hills to the east.

As Brian maneuvered the unmarked police car into the parking lot at the top of the hill, Blake marveled at all of the tourists milling about, snapping photos of the panoramic view and pointing out distant landmarks. Market Street lay far below, winding its way slowly up the hill. Downtown San Francisco seemed to shimmer in the distance. The East Bay stretched out beyond a lone cargo ship that crept along. "Jesus," he said, peering out the window. "At least three tourist buses are up here."

"You afraid somebody will recognize you?" Brian asked.

"No. I'm afraid somebody will see me talking to thin air and think I'm nuts."

Melody laughed from the backseat. "It wouldn't be the first time."

"Don't worry," Brian said. "The spot we're looking for is just over there, out of sight."

As he led Blake and Melody to the place where the body of Ms. Cho was discovered, he explained that numerous forestry employees had reported "something odd" about it, and the story quickly spread that the area was haunted. The interesting thing was that none of the forestry employees knew of the area's history or that a body had been found there decades earlier. As they rounded a rocky mound covered with brush and wild sage, Blake was happy to be away from the crowds of tourists.

"Right over there," Brian whispered, his tone almost reverent. "That's where they found Betsy Cho and where people have reported strange occurrences."

"What sort of 'occurrences'?" Melody asked.

"Cold spots, strange, disembodied voices, even tossed stones."

Blake suppressed the urge to point out that high atop Twin Peaks—even on the warmest days—cold spots didn't sound that unusual. Even the disembodied voices could be attributed to voices emanating from the surrounding houses, carried on the wind. Still, the fact people had gone to the trouble of reporting these things—coupled with the coincidence of the location—made Blake hold his tongue.

"Do you sense anything?" he asked, turning to Melody.

Melody, who had remained standing beside Brian, was quiet for a moment.

"No. But it's a very unhappy place."

Blake turned back to the spot, facing west. Funny, he thought as he gazed out over the Sunset District toward the Pacific, that this could be considered an unhappy place. Nevertheless, he wanted to help Brian solve the case, if only to prove his chief wrong. He half closed his eyes, focusing his gaze across the dusty path. Suddenly, a man appeared on the path. He was wearing seventies-style clothing, and the only part of him visible was from the waist up. The spirit instantly stopped, hovering in midair and staring at them.

"Who are you?" he asked, his eyes narrowed. "How can you see me?"

"We're looking for a ghost, one that's been causing trouble up here. Is it you?"

The phantom smiled in a twisted, evil manner but didn't answer.

"Did you know Betsy Cho?"

The spirit became visibly irritated at the mention of the name and averted his gaze to a clump of bushes to his right.

"Did you kill her?" Goose bumps suddenly covered Blake's arms.

The spirit suddenly seemed to recover from his shock and smiled again.

"And the others? Did you kill them, too?"

"Bitches," the ghost hissed.

Blake felt he was truly in the presence of evil. "Does your name begin with a J?" he asked, undaunted.

"Idiot," the ghost spat, "my name is Jay!"

Brian, who had been standing at a distance beside Melody, nervously cleared his throat.

"Blake," he asked hesitantly, "who are you talking to?"

"We found the Doodler."

❖

Despite Blake's efforts to extract additional information from the spirit, the name Jay was all he was willing to offer.

As Brian maneuvered the car back down the hill, he cursed loudly. "How the hell am I supposed to tell the chief that we found the Doodler, but, oh, by the way, he's dead now?"

Blake thought for a moment. "Well," he said finally, "he must have died up there, too. Surely there would be records of a man named Jay who died on Twin Peaks."

Brian was silent.

Melody chimed in from the backseat. "After the last known killing."

"I don't know," Brian said. "It doesn't sound like much to go on."

The car fell silent as they continued back to the police station. Brian was angry at himself for not feeling even the slightest bit of elation over the news that the Doodler was dead, but what was he supposed to tell the chief? As he parked in his spot on the police lot, he turned to Blake.

"I'm sorry," he said. "I'm just not sure how the chief will take this new information. He's not exactly the most tolerant person when it comes to this sort of thing."

"Then we'll get him evidence. Don't mention what we saw up there. Not yet."

Brian nodded, kissed Blake lightly on the cheek, and got out of the car. Blake and Melody shared a brief, knowing look before they followed him.

The records department of the SFPD was massive and meticulously maintained. Blake and Melody waited as Brian requested copies of old police reports, beginning the week of the last known murder. He returned with a stack of manila folders, each one three inches thick, and directed his guests to an empty table against a far wall.

"Here," he passed a random folder to Blake and then one to Melody, "we might as well get started."

Blake looked across the table at his boyfriend. Brian was so level-headed and sure of himself. Blake couldn't help but feel slightly aroused as he watched him in action. He suggestively nudged Brian's leg under the table but Brian, engrossed in the contents of the folder in front of him, ignored the flirting. Blake sighed and opened his own folder, reading reports of crimes committed before he was even born. Rapes, murders, assaults, burglaries. The aging reports in front of Blake ran the gamut of human evils. How could people be so callous to other human beings? After a mere ten minutes of perusing the folders, Melody gasped. Both Brian and Blake looked up from their own folders, expectantly. With wide eyes, she pushed a page toward them.

The report in question was classified Hit and Run, with the fatality listed as Jay Dean Mitchell, thirty-five, of 411 Crestline. No witnesses to the incident were listed, which occurred three days after the last murder known to have been committed by the Doodler.

"Holy shit." Brian reread the report. "Crestline is on Twin Peaks."

"So the other psychics were right," Melody said. "He did live nearby."

"Still, this doesn't prove our ghost is the Doodler."

"But he is. He practically confessed as much to Blake."

"But how do we prove it? As far as everyone else is concerned, this is just some poor guy who got hit by a car."

"The report says that Mr. Mitchell lived on Crestline with his mother," Blake said. "If she's still living maybe she can help us out."

Brian silently considered his suggestion for a moment before rising from his seat, the report in hand. "I'll be right back," he said, then walked briskly from the room.

"This is right, I know it," Melody whispered, once she was certain he was gone.

"I agree, but…"

Brian re-entered the room holding a photocopy of the original report. After replacing the original report he silently gathered up the remaining folders and took the stack back to the captain behind the counter. Blake and Melody remained silent, even when Brian returned to the table and sat down.

"Here's the deal," he said, staring at his hands. "I think we're onto something and, according to the records, Jay's mother still lives at the house on Crestline. But we can't barge into his mother's house without a search warrant—"

"So get a search warrant," Melody said.

Brian held up a hand to silence her.

"We can't get one based on the evidence at hand."

Once again they fell silent and Brian stared wistfully at the photocopied police report.

This time Blake broke the silence. "I have an idea."

Brian and Melody looked at him expectantly.

"Just drive us up there and I'll explain on the way."

The plan was brilliant in its simplicity, although Brian still had misgivings after Blake went over it. He would simply introduce himself, explain to Mrs. Mitchell her son's ghost had appeared to him, and Brian could look around for evidence while Blake kept her preoccupied.

"Still," Brian said, "it's been over twenty years since the murders. I don't know what kind of evidence you expect me to find."

The houses perched on Crestline seemed to cling unnaturally to the steep hills, as if one strong breeze would send them all crashing to the valley below. They were similar in design, with minor differences here and there as if to set them apart from their neighboring houses. Where space allowed, eucalyptus and bald cypress trees clung to the earth. Blake imagined they would still be rooted to their spots long after the houses were gone.

411 Crestline was an unassuming two-story stucco abode, set into the side of the hill. Similar in appearance and style to the neighboring houses, it easily blended in, made unique only by the street number above the door. Brian parked on the street in front of the house and they made their way up the steps. After they quickly knocked on the door they could hear a deadbolt being released and a short, graying woman in her seventies appeared.

"Yes?" she asked, obviously surprised by visitors.

"Mrs. Mitchell?" Brian asked.

"Yes?"

"I'm Brian Cox with the San Francisco Police Department." He showed her his badge. "I have someone who wants to speak with you."

Blake stepped forward and extended his hand. "Mrs. Mitchell, I'm—"

"Blake Danzig," she said, a twinkle in her eyes. "Why, I watch your television show all the time! What in the world?"

"May we come in?" Blake asked.

"Heavens, yes." Mrs. Mitchell stepped aside to allow entry. "Where are my manners? Please," she gestured to a sofa and some armchairs, "make yourselves comfortable."

Blake looked around the cozy living room and the unmistakable furnishings of an elderly grandmother. Lace curtains covered a large bay window facing the street, a comfortable-looking chintz sofa was flanked by two over-stuffed armchairs and porcelain figurines lined a shelf on the wall. He hoped they were wrong, but when he spied a photo of Jay on the wall leading into the kitchen, chills ran down his spine.

"Mrs. Mitchell," he said, turning to her, "I'm here about your son."

Mrs. Mitchell looked confused and her eyes moistened. "You mean Jay? He's been dead for over twenty years now."

"I know." Blake touched her arm. "He contacted me."

Blake took a seat on the sofa next to the perplexed woman and explained his encounter on Twin Peaks, careful to omit any references to the murders. When he finished, Mrs. Mitchell walked to the wall and removed the framed photograph Blake had already seen. She touched the glass lovingly and offered it to Blake. He hesitantly accepted the photo and stared into the eyes of the man he knew was the Doodler. The man looked like a typical thirtysomething—happy, healthy, and well-dressed. He could have been anyone, a nameless face on the street, with nondescript hair, a long face with a pointed chin, and blue eyes hidden behind silver-rimmed glasses. He passed the photo to Melody, who seemed visibly shaken when she held it. She hastily passed the photo to Brian.

"I'm not surprised you saw my Jay up there on the peaks," Mrs. Mitchell said, accepting the photo back from Brian and replacing it on the wall. "He loved to go running up there at night. He was so into keeping fit."

Blake and Brian exchanged a quick look, then Blake turned back to Mrs. Mitchell.

"Didn't he think it was unsafe to go running up there at night?" he asked.

"I warned him all the time," she replied, wistfully, "but he assured me he would be all right because he wore light clothing so that cars could see him in the dark…"

"Mrs. Mitchell," Blake said, "did you happen to keep any of your son's belongings?"

She stared at him, seeming confused.

"If I could touch something that belonged to him…" Perspiration was beginning to form under his arms.

"Well, of course," she said, finally understanding. "I kept his room just like he left it. I never changed a thing."

Chapter Five

The journals recovered from Jay Dean Mitchell's room, hidden in a box in the back of his closet, proved conclusively that he had been the killer known as the Doodler. Not only did his handwriting match that on the drawings left at the crime scenes, but he had kept samples of hair from his victims and carefully labeled each one. Major newspapers across the country announced the news and applauded the SFPD for solving the two-decades-old case. No mention was made in the media of Blake's involvement. The official story was that Jay Dean Mitchell was being investigated as another possible victim of the killer, based on his unsolved death at the hands of a hit-and-run driver around the time of the murders. Mrs. Mitchell—broken and humiliated—agreed not to speak to the press about the visit from the famous ghost hunter. And Blake, while happy about helping to solve the case, couldn't help but feel guilty about tricking Mrs. Mitchell.

"But he was a murderer," Brian said, exasperation creeping into his voice, "one of the worst in California history!" He jumped up from the bed and began to dress, not wanting to argue.

"I know," Blake replied. "But she wasn't. And for twenty-odd years she believed her son was a good person who was simply killed by a hit-and-run driver. I helped ruin that memory, possibly speeding up that old woman's death."

"Oh, come on." Brian turned away from Blake. "You don't believe that, do you?"

"She's old," Blake replied sadly. "Now I doubt if even her neighbors will speak to her."

"That's not your problem." Brian pulled on his shirt. "You were just helping us solve a case."

Blake nodded, but couldn't get Mrs. Mitchell's face out of his head. She made him miss his own parents, now retired to a small town outside Albuquerque after they sold the Danzig Brothers Circus to a larger conglomerate. He said so to Brian, who sighed loudly and stopped putting his clothes on.

"Maybe you should go visit them," he said, sitting down on the bed where Blake was lying. He tenderly kissed him on the forehead. "A trip might make you feel better."

Blake sighed.

"I can't." He propped himself up on his elbows. "I'm scheduled to film some segments of the show for FX this weekend in Los Angeles."

"Oh." Brian looked crestfallen. "When did you intend to tell me that?"

"I thought I did." Seeing the look on Brian's face, he said, "Jesus. It's my job."

Blake jumped out of bed and walked into the adjoining bathroom. Brian admired his hairy, muscular ass as he crossed the room, and shook his head. Brian put on his tie. He was grabbing his jacket from the back of an armchair when Blake re-emerged from the bathroom and pulled on the pair of boxer shorts he had earlier discarded on the floor.

"Look," he said, taking Brian in his arms. "I'm sorry if

I forgot to tell you about this weekend. Why don't you come down with me?"

"I can't." Brian kissed him lightly on the lips. "I have to attend a police seminar in Oakland this weekend."

Blake nodded and stooped to pick up a discarded T-shirt. "We're not working out, are we?" he asked, without making eye contact.

"No." The word caught in Brian's throat.

"What can I do?" Blake sat on the edge of the bed and looked up at him. "I'll do whatever you want."

Brian sat next to Blake and put a hand on his leg. "We're just too different," he said hesitantly. "You travel a lot, which I understand, and then there's the whole ghost thing."

"The 'ghost thing' used to freak me out, too, Brian, but it's who I am. I can't help it."

"It's just weird, waking up in the middle of the night, hearing you whispering to people who aren't even there. Sometimes I feel like I'm going crazy."

Blake laughed. Not a forced, angry laugh, but a sincere, heartfelt laugh. Midnight, the time between day and night, had always been a difficult time for him because of the number of ghosts active. It wasn't as bad as Halloween, but close. "I'm sorry about that," he said, arising from the bed. "I know how creepy that must be. But can we try to work this out? I really like you, Brian."

Brian slowly nodded, then rose, embracing Blake. "We'll talk when you get back from LA."

As Brian left the apartment, Blake couldn't help but wonder if he had just left for good.

❖

For most of their southbound flight, Blake sat lost in silent contemplation. Melody, who was seated next to him reading a magazine, finally nudged him and asked, "Are you all right?"

"I'm fine. I was just thinking about Brian."

"Listen, Brian's a good guy and everything, but if it doesn't work out, it doesn't work out."

Blake looked at her with what felt like a hangdog expression.

"I'm just saying, you haven't known each other that long and at least you haven't moved in together yet."

"This from a lesbian." Blake felt better—good enough to tease her. "How does it go? Rent a U-Haul after the second date?"

Melody playfully slapped his arm with the rolled-up magazine. "Well, this lesbian hasn't seen any action in months," she groaned, "so I wouldn't know."

❖

Blake had never had a great opinion of Los Angeles, considering the city too reliant on cars and plastic surgeons, although he viewed Hollywood with an almost childlike nostalgia. Hollywood Boulevard, however, reminded him what he was attracted to wasn't real, like it was produced for him like a movie flickering on a big screen, doing its best with a song and a dance to hide the decay of the neglected buildings, the parade of lost souls, living and dead, which wandered its length and breadth. For decades, so many people had come here searching for a dream that was never fulfilled, had worked here and died here, and the evidence was all around him. The teenaged runaways, sitting in doorways and begging for money; the faded actor, who nobody would hire because of his drinking; the screenwriter, who hadn't had a fresh idea in five years—they, too, were the living dead, passing time until they were ghosts like Montgomery Clift and Marilyn.

The studio car picked them up at the airport and drove them directly to the Hollywood Roosevelt Hotel. Not only were they staying there, but they'd be filming their latest paranormal investigation there. Situated on Hollywood Boulevard, across the street from Grauman's Chinese Theater, the Hollywood Roosevelt had opened in 1927 and was the site of the first Academy Awards banquet in 1929. A plethora of stars of the golden age stayed there over the years, and some refused to leave even after their death. Marilyn Monroe, Montgomery Clift, Clark Gable, and a dozen other spirits were said to haunt the venerable old hotel. The *Haunted California* team was there to film a segment to be aired for Halloween. Because of the number of supposed spirits concentrated there, the producers decided to focus solely on the Roosevelt and ignore other nearby haunted hotels and theaters. This was fine with Blake, since it made his job easier. Besides, he reasoned, they could always come back to the other locales later, for future episodes of the show.

After checking in at the front desk, Blake turned to Melody. "I'm going to call Brian and let him know we got here okay."

He walked across to a grouping of overstuffed chairs in a corner of the lobby and pulled out his cell phone, dialing the now-familiar number. His call went directly into Brian's voice mail. Though Blake was slightly miffed, he tried not to convey his annoyance in his message.

"Hi, Brian," he said. "I just wanted to let you know we arrived safely. Give me a call later, okay?" He snapped his cell phone shut and returned to Melody, who was waiting for him beside the front counter.

"I got his voice mail," he said, answering the expectant expression on Melody's face. "Probably still at that conference."

Melody merely nodded, gazing across the garish Spanish-style lobby. The floors were covered by large tiles and, looking down upon them like sentries, ornate balconies peeked from beneath the painted, beamed ceilings. A fountain gurgled in the middle of the room, barely audible over the echoing footsteps of the other guests.

"This place is wild," she said, pointing at the ornately painted ceiling. Blake appreciated that Melody was trying to change the subject, but didn't say anything.

"Well," he replied, "I've already seen a couple of apparitions walk through here in period clothing. Then again," he said, "this is Hollywood, so it could have been someone in costume."

"So, what's the deal with this hotel?"

"Supposedly, Marilyn Monroe and Montgomery Clift haunt this place. We're staying on the ninth floor, which Monty is said to haunt."

"I want to run into Marilyn." Melody licked her lips suggestively.

"Why do you think I wanted to stay on the ninth floor? I wouldn't mind running into Montgomery Clift, ghost or not."

CHAPTER SIX

The producers of *Haunted California* rented out the entire ninth floor in the hopes of catching a glimpse of the ghost of Montgomery Clift. Blake decided to sleep in room number 928, said to be where Clift stayed back in 1953 while preparing for his role in the movie *From Here to Eternity*. The countless reports of activity in the room ranged from a shadowy specter sitting in a chair in the corner to loud bugle blasts in the hall, reminiscent of Clift's stay there when, in preparation for his role, he practiced playing the bugle. Many of the hotel's staff flatly refused to work on the ninth floor, citing a "weird energy." That was the official story, anyway.

Blake opened the door to the room slowly because he didn't want to displace any energy by barging in. Melody, whose room was directly across the hall, stood behind him watching.

Blake looked at the nondescript room, almost disappointed. It was hard to believe that this room, now updated to look like any other hotel room in any other city in the world, had ever been used by a great actor like Montgomery Clift. The new floral bedspread, the upholstered chair, the whole thing shouted to Blake that it was anything but 1953. The furnishings—flat, sterile, plain—were almost an insult to the room where the great actor had slept. Even the white walls seemed to say to Blake, "Who cares?"

"See anything?" Melody whispered, after a moment's hesitation.

"No, at least not right now."

He tossed his bag onto the bed and beckoned for Melody to enter. "Do you sense anything?"

Melody stepped hesitantly into the room and peered from side to side. She closed her eyes and slowly shook her head. "No. It feels a little creepy in here, though. I don't know." She plopped down on the bed next to Blake. "Maybe we'll get something later, when it gets dark."

"I hope so. I'd really love to talk to Monty. What a handsome guy."

"Really?" Melody had a smile on her face. "Didn't he have a funny eye or something?"

"He was in a car accident! But, yeah, I think he was very handsome."

The star of movies like *From Here to Eternity*, *The Young Lions*, and *The Misfits*, Montgomery Clift had been involved in a car accident in 1956 during the filming of *Raintree County*. As a result of his injuries, including a broken nose, broken jaw, and lacerations, he began to drink heavily, which adversely affected his career.

"Well, I'm on the lookout for Marilyn." Melody rose from the bed. "And I think I'll go change into something a little more presentable in case we bump into her."

"I wouldn't mind bumping into Marilyn, either," Blake replied, "although for entirely different reasons from your own."

"You gay boys love your Hollywood starlets. Meet me in the lobby in fifteen minutes?"

Blake quickly changed shirts and checked his cell phone for a missed call from Brian. He sighed and put his bag into the closet.

Perhaps Melody was right. At least they hadn't invested too much time in their relationship. Still, if it was over, Blake wanted to hear it from Brian.

Blake closed and locked his door. The network had hired security guards to cordon off the ninth floor from the public, but, he figured, it was better safe than sorry. Downstairs in the lobby, he strode across the tiled floor to the gurgling fountain in the middle of the room. As he looked at the people around him, some with suitcases, most with cameras, he wondered which of them might really be a ghost. Sometimes it was impossible to tell the difference. He was just about to turn and walk to a staircase leading to the basement when the voice of a child stopped him. He turned, and standing before him was a little girl in a pink sweater and blue jeans. She appeared to be no more than five or six years old and had her brown hair pulled back in a ponytail. She looked as if she had been crying.

"Hello," Blake said, crouching down in front of her. "Where's your mommy?"

"I don't know. I can't find her."

"Don't worry, we'll find her."

He stood up and held out his hand but, instead of taking it, the little girl vanished in midair.

❖

That afternoon, while Blake, Melody, and the show's producer, Marty, met with the hotel manager, Blake mentioned the little girl.

"That was Caroline," the manager replied. "She's one of our regular spirits and has been seen around the hotel for years now."

Blake laughed and shook his head. "No matter how many times I encounter ghosts, I still have trouble identifying them right away."

The manager, a handsome, well-dressed man in his early forties named Donald, smiled. "You'll have plenty of opportunities to see ghosts here."

He explained that in addition to Caroline, Marilyn, and Montgomery, ghostly encounters had been reported in the boiler room, the Academy Room, and the Blossom Room, site of the first Academy Awards banquet, among others.

"We'll set up cameras in all those rooms," Marty, the show's producer, suggested.

Already famous for the scores of shows he had produced in the past, Marty was pure Hollywood. A corpulent man of only five-eight, Marty wore flashy suits with Italian labels and drove a shiny sports car. He was most often recognized for his hair, however, a curly mass of thick gray pushed back to conceal an obvious bald spot. He seemed to take everything in good humor and always be relaxed, no matter the situation.

"That's fine," Donald said. "I've instructed my staff to do everything necessary to accommodate your needs."

Blake expressed his appreciation, then said, "Would it be possible to have a tour of the hotel before we begin taping?"

"Of course. I'll have my assistant, Kyle, show you around."

Kyle met Blake and Melody in the lobby ten minutes later. He was tall, around six-one, with a head full of dark, curly hair and penetrating blue eyes. His skin was unblemished and pale as alabaster. He grasped Blake's hand enthusiastically as he introduced himself to them.

"Mr. Danzig," he said warmly, "I'm a huge fan of your show…a huge fan."

"Thanks. But, please, call me Blake."

He led them to the elevator and pressed a button. "I'm taking you to the penthouse first, where Clark Gable and Carole Lombard stayed when they were here."

As the elevator carried them to the top of the hotel, Kyle addressed Blake. "So, I hear you're staying in Monty's room."

"That's correct. I hear there have been a lot of odd occurrences in that room."

"You name it. Telephones left off of the hook when the room was empty, calls to the front desk when nobody was staying in that room, apparitions, and even one guest who claimed something lay on top of him while he was in the bed."

"Have you ever seen Monty's ghost?"

"No. I wish."

Melody sighed loudly and Blake playfully nudged her.

The penthouse suite was an opulent affair, with high beamed ceilings and its own kitchenette. The living room alone was bigger than Blake's entire apartment, and the room's decorations were decidedly masculine, befitting Clark Gable. Kyle pointed to a door and explained it led to a neighboring room where Ms. Lombard "officially" stayed, since she was having an affair with the very married Mr. Gable. "At that time," he said, "this room ran for about five dollars per night."

From the penthouse, they rode the elevator back to the

lobby, where Kyle pointed out the tiled stairs where Shirley Temple learned to tap dance. He then took them into the Blossom Room where the first Academy Awards banquet was held. As they entered, a gust of cold air escaped and goose bumps covered Blake's whole body. Although the room wasn't without its surviving Art Deco touches, it still had the overall appearance of almost any hotel conference room, complete with standard folding tables and uncomfortable chairs. But the air in the room buzzed with paranormal energy.

Kyle said, "The first awards ceremony—"

"Wait." Blake lifted a hand to silence him. "Sorry," he explained. "This room is full of spirits."

Unseen to all but him was a ghostly long table in the middle of the room, surrounded by fifteen spirits, all dressed in 1920s fashion. The spirits looked up at them as if they had just interrupted a very important meeting.

"Excuse us," Blake said, and turned back to his companions, excitement building in him. "We definitely have to record in this room tonight."

As Kyle led them out to the poolside suites, Blake explained what he had seen.

"I sensed great anxiety in the room," Melody said, "maybe even anger."

"I wonder if I was seeing the spirits relive the first Academy Awards banquet?"

"Could be. Maybe I was picking up on the anxiety of one of the actors awaiting the envelope?"

Blake and Kyle both laughed at Melody's unintentional joke, then they suddenly stopped in front of one of the poolside bungalows. "The painting on the bottom of the pool was done by Hockney," Kyle said, gesturing to the swimming pool.

Blake and Melody admired the underwater mural, made up of hundreds of blue crescents that created a dazzling effect under the blue water. Although the artwork wasn't exactly to Blake's taste, he nodded appreciatively.

"Marilyn Monroe's first advertising gig was a photography session here." Kyle pointed to the diving board. "And this bungalow was where she stayed."

Melody's face brightened. "Have people seen her ghost in there?"

Kyle laughed at her obvious enthusiasm and unlocked the door, which led into a very spacious and tastefully decorated room. A four-poster bed, draped with white fabric, sat in the middle of the room. Sunlight poured in from the windows and played across the carpeted floor, seeming to reach for the stuffed chair that sat in a corner. Being in there somehow made Blake feel like he was at the ocean.

"There have been some things that couldn't be explained," Kyle replied, "but her ghost is said to appear in a mirror that used to hang in this room."

"Where's the mirror now?" Melody asked.

Blake chuckled. Was she honestly hoping for a tryst with a spirit? Was that even possible?

"The mirror is in the lower lobby," Kyle said, "beside the elevator. I planned to show that to you next, on the way to the boiler room."

Melody stared at her surroundings for a moment, apparently waiting for a reading.

"Anything?" Blake asked.

"Happiness. I sense happiness in this room."

"Me, too. But I don't see her."

"Maybe in the mirror," Kyle suggested.

Back inside the hotel Kyle led the way down a short flight of stairs, stopping beside an elevator. On the wall beside the doors hung a large colonial-style, wood-framed mirror.

"This is it?" Melody sounded disappointed.

Blake, however, smiled and said, "Hello, Marilyn."

The familiar blonde reflected in the glass smiled coquettishly back at him.

❖

All the episodes of *Haunted California* were filmed using simple handheld cameras and, unlike similar shows, they kept the overhead lights on instead of filming the scenes in night vision. The one bit of gadgetry they did use was sensitive recording equipment, for picking up EVPs, or Electronic Voice Phenomena. The taping went very well, capturing a shadowy image of a man in the swimming pool invisible to the naked eye, the ghostly image of a man in a white suit in the lobby, a dark vortex in the Blossom Room, strange orbs in the boiler room, and an eerie gold light emanating from the "Marilyn mirror." Unfortunately, no spirit materialized in the Montgomery Clift room.

As the crew wrapped up taping for the night and stowed away the equipment, Melody approached Blake, yawning. "I'm beat," she said. "Are you going up to your room?"

"No. We got a lot of good stuff tonight. I'm going to have a celebratory drink in the bar."

"Good night, then. I'll see you in the morning."

"Good night."

Blake walked to the entrance to a bar just off the lobby. The vaulted ceilings danced with the light of candles placed at various intervals, and he took a seat at the nearly empty bar. He ordered a glass of wine from the bartender and had just taken his first sip when he was surprised by a voice behind him.

"Mind if I join you?"

He turned to see Kyle standing behind him, his untied necktie hanging around his neck.

"No, please." Blake motioned to the empty bar stool next to his.

Kyle ordered a glass of wine for himself and turned to Blake. "So," he said, raising his glass for a toast, "it sounds like you had a good show tonight."

"We did. But I was disappointed that Monty never showed up."

"Maybe he's shy. Besides, you'll be sleeping in that room all night, and the night's still young."

Blake nodded and took a sip of his wine.

"You want some company?" Kyle lightly rubbed his leg against Blake's.

"Um, Kyle, I don't know if that's a good idea."

"I'm sorry. I thought…"

He cleared his throat. "Really. I'm sorry. So…are you in a relationship?"

Blake thought for a moment. Brian still hadn't returned his call from that morning. "No." He rose from the bar stool and tossed back the remains of his wine. "Come on. I'd love some company."

Chapter Seven

For Blake, the flight back to San Francisco was difficult. He didn't want to confront Brian and deal with what he knew was inevitable. As usual, Melody was supportive of whatever Blake did and kept assuring him he had done nothing wrong. Still, despite the fact Brian had failed to call during his three days in Los Angeles, Blake felt guilty. At least he'd had the good sense to be safe.

"And the whole night, no Montgomery Clift?" Melody whispered, leaning close.

"No. Unfortunately not."

"Not that you would have noticed." Melody laughed. "I could hear you boys from across the hall."

Despite his guilt, Blake couldn't help but laugh with her. If Monty had been in the room he would have gotten quite a show, with Blake's meaty cock shoved up Kyle's willing asshole. Not that having a ghost in the room during sex would have been a new experience for Blake, but the idea of Montgomery Clift watching him in action was definitely a turn-on.

"Let's hope he wasn't there," Blake said.

Suddenly, the voice of the captain announcing their arrival

in San Francisco snapped Blake back to reality. He looked out the window at the bay that seemed to rise to greet them as they approached the runway.

❖

The airport taxi dropped Blake off at his apartment before it took Melody to the Mission District. Blake rode the elevator to his condo, suitcase in hand, and let himself into his apartment. The answering machine on the small table beside the door announced that he had messages. He pressed the button to play them back and was disappointed that the only ones were from Donatella and Marty. Suddenly angry, he dialed Brian's cell phone.

Brian answered on the second ring. "Hey," he said, nonchalantly, "are you still in LA?"

"No." Blake did his best to mask his frustration and keep his voice level. "I just got back this afternoon."

"How did it go?"

"Fine. Brian, why didn't you call me?"

"I'm sorry." Brian sighed. "I was really busy with the conference this weekend and didn't get in until late."

"For three days?" Irritation was finally creeping into Blake's voice. "You still could have called."

"Blake, I—"

Blake surprised himself by cutting Brian off. "Brian," he said determinedly, "are we a couple or not? I have to know— yes or no—so I can move on with my life."

"Blake, it's not that simple. I mean, I still feel the way I did, and I do care about you."

"But you don't love me?"

When there was no response from the other end of the line, Blake could feel his face flush. "I'll take that as a no."

Brian ignored Blake's comment. "Can we have dinner?"

Blake wanted to say no, go to hell, to tell him about Kyle just to hurt him, but, instead, he calmed, just wanting to see Brian. "Sure," he said, "meet me at my apartment at seven and we'll walk down to Rue Lepic."

"That sounds good." Brian hung up.

Filled with conflicting emotions, Blake tossed his phone onto the counter and began to undress so that he could shower. He turned on the water and, once it was a comfortable temperature, climbed in, letting it caress his body. Should he tell Brian the truth? He wasn't sure. To do so might mean the end of their relationship, but Blake hated the idea of keeping a secret from the man he wanted to spend his life with. And Blake Danzig was no liar.

Brian arrived at the Nob Hill apartment exactly at seven o'clock. Blake greeted him at the door, dressed in jeans and a gray T-shirt. Though he had rehearsed what he wanted to say to Brian all morning, seeing his sandy-haired, green-eyed boyfriend standing in front of him caused him to forget everything. And he was still wearing his tight slacks and a tie, slightly loosened.

"I missed you," he said, instead, kissing Brian.

As they embraced, they came alive and their kisses became passionate, tongues exploring each other's mouths. With shaking hands they grappled with buttons, belts, and ties and were soon naked on the living-room floor. Blake glimpsed their bodies in the full-length mirror on the nearby wall, an image that always turned him on. The sight of his dark, hairy body coupled with Brian's smooth, pale one was beautiful, and Blake groaned as Brian took his cock into his mouth.

"Brian," he moaned, "wait. We need to talk about something."

"Shh." Brian got up and placed a finger over Blake's moist lips. "Not now," he said. "I want you to fuck my ass, baby. Fuck me until I can't walk. Please."

"But—"

Brian silenced Blake by rising to his knees and pushing his stiff cock against his mouth, a meaty temptation Blake had no strength to ignore. He took Brian's boner into his mouth and swallowed it until Brian's pubes were against his face.

"Fuck, yeah," Brian said, "swallow that meat, baby. Fuck, I've missed your hot body."

Blake sucked hungrily on Brian's meaty tool and fingered Brian's asshole.

"Yeah," Brian groaned, "play with my hole. Get it ready for your big, uncut dick."

Suddenly, Brian pulled his cock out of Blake's mouth, a large drop of pre-come dripping from his piss slit.

"Not too fast, baby," he said, breathing heavily. "I don't want to get off yet."

He stood up and offered a hand to Blake, helping him rise from the floor, and led him into the bedroom. As he leaned over the bedside table to get a condom, Blake took advantage of his position to rim the muscular ass.

"Shit," Brian whispered, "my cock's ready to explode. That feels good, baby. Yeah, eat my ass."

Blake licked hungrily at the pink asshole and thrust his tongue in and out as if he was starving to death. His own cock was rock-hard and pointing up from between his hairy legs, and he stroked it sparingly, gently, not wanting to come by jacking off. He wanted Brian's ass.

He stood up behind his lover and lavished kisses on his neck and back and reached around to tug on Brian's hard, pink nipples.

Brian's whole body was covered in goose bumps and he shivered as he reached around to slide the greasy condom onto Blake's stiff cock. Blake's cock throbbed at the sudden sensation of tightness around it, almost as if it had its own heartbeat.

"Put some lube on your ass," Blake whispered in Brian's ear.

Brian retrieved a bottle from the drawer and squirted some of the cold liquid onto Blake's hot, throbbing dick, then smeared more of the gel onto his wet asshole.

Blake guided his stiff cock toward Brian's waiting hole, gently pushing his throbbing dick into the tight, primed asshole. Both of them exhaled loudly as the boner inched along and finally pressed deeply into Brian. Blake stood motionless for a moment, relishing the sensation of being far inside his lover.

Brian, his prostate fully stimulated, felt almost light-headed. A large stream of pre-come dripped from the head of his cock and landed on top of the bedside table.

"Shit," he managed to mutter, enjoying the sensation of having his ass filled with fat cock. "You feel so fucking good."

Blake tugged at Brian's nipples and began to fuck his ass, slowly at first, but then gradually increasing the frequency of his strokes. The sounds of their naked bodies slapping together, coupled with the smells of the lube, pre-come, and sweaty bodies, was driving Blake crazy, and he plowed Brian's willing ass with zeal. Suddenly, Brian's asshole tightened around his cock.

"Fuck," Brian gasped, "I'm coming."

He shot a large, white load, which hit the wall above the bedside table. Coaxed by the tightened hole, Blake blew his load in Brian's ass and filled up the condom.

Sweaty and out of breath, they collapsed onto the bed and held each other tight.

"I do love you, you know," Brian finally managed to say, his face buried in Blake's hairy chest.

"I know," Blake replied, suddenly feeling guilty again. "I...I love you, too."

Blake propped himself up on his elbows and looked at Brian. "You want to shower before dinner?" He tried to shake off the mental image of Kyle's naked body.

"I guess we should." Brian laughed. "We smell like sex."

Blake got up from the bed and walked into the adjacent bathroom, where he turned on the shower. Brian, his boner not yet subsided, followed him.

Freshly showered and dressed, they walked the short distance down Mason Street to Rue Lepic, a small French restaurant located on the corner. The restaurant sat just below the top of Nob Hill, below the grand, old hotels at its peak and at the foot of a very steep hill. On either side of it were apartment buildings situated on tree-lined streets, and Blake loved how quaint and intimate the small space felt.

Fortunately, the place wasn't crowded and so they were quickly seated. After ordering a bottle of wine and an appetizer from the handsome young waiter, Brian took Blake's hand. "I'm sorry I didn't call when you were in LA."

"Brian—" The waiter returned with their bottle of wine, and they were silent as he opened the bottle and offered Blake a sample.

"It's fine, thank you."

The waiter filled both glasses and winked at Blake. "I love your show," he whispered before scurrying away.

Brian laughed, but Blake was grateful for the waiter's discretion.

"That's part of my problem with 'us,'" Brian said, not unkindly. "When you travel, I bet you've got guys all over you."

Blake flushed, and he fidgeted with his wineglass before looking Brian squarely in the eye. "That's what I wanted to talk to you about." His heart was pounding.

Brian didn't reply, but stared at Blake expectantly.

"I had sex with a guy in LA. A guy who works at the hotel where we stayed."

Brian's face went pale and he stared blankly at Blake. "When were you going to tell me?" he asked, his voice low.

"I tried, earlier. But then we had sex, and…"

Brian looked at his glass, then back at Blake. "Blake," he said, moving his hand back across the table, "this is all my fault. I should have called you back, but—"

"But what, Brian?"

"Blake, I love you, I do, but I'm not sure I'm the right guy for you."

Blake's throat constricted and he couldn't speak.

❖

A week later, Brian finally called Blake and said he wanted to remain friends. He wondered if they could meet in Golden Gate Park to talk. Blake agreed, but felt sad that Brian had chosen a public place. Nevertheless, this was one way to gain closure, so he went, meeting Brian by the fountain across from the aquarium.

"How are you?" Brian asked, cautiously hugging him.

"I'm fine, thanks. You?"

"Good. I've been really busy at work."

Blake sensed that Brian was lying. After a couple of minutes of silence that seemed like an eternity, he asked, "Why did you want to see me, Brian?"

While he generally appreciated people who got right to the point, Brian looked slightly irritated that Blake seemed to be in such a hurry. He gestured to a nearby park bench and they sat down. Pigeons milled around the fountain and a wayward seagull begged scraps of bread from nearby tourists eating their lunch. The sun was shining brightly overhead, and Blake suddenly became aware of a spirit, a man in a tweed suit, standing beside the fountain. More interested in what Brian had to say, however, he diverted his gaze away from the ghost. The spirit could wait. Blake looked at Brian expectantly.

"Blake," Brian said, "I'm not mad at you about the guy in LA. That was my fault for leaving things the way I did. The truth is, I'm not sure if I'm ready to be in a steady relationship."

Blake sighed and looked back at the fountain. The spirit was still there.

"Thank you." Blake looked back at Brian. "I appreciate that."

"I guess we weren't meant to be together. I mean, the ghost stuff and all…it just scares the hell out of me."

"I can't help who I am, Brian," Blake said softly. He

glanced back at the spirit, if only to lessen the pain he was feeling as he looked at Brian's sweet face.

"I know that. I don't want you to change. I just can't be around the ghost thing twenty-four hours a day."

He followed Blake's gaze toward the fountain. "You're looking at one of them right now, aren't you?"

"Yes."

"That's what I'm talking about. I don't want to know there's a ghost around every corner. I love you…I really do, but I'm just not the right guy for you."

"I wish I was something other than what I am." Tears welled in Blake's eyes.

"Don't," Brian said, taking Blake's hand. "You're a wonderful, kind person. This…this fear I have of the unknown…it's my problem. Hell, Blake, I carry a gun to fight criminals. You face things I could never face, making you ten times the hero I am. Don't ever change who you are."

"I'll always love you," Blake whispered, a knot in his throat.

"Me, too."

They embraced and held each other for a very long time. Finally, Blake pulled away. His phone rang and he looked at the screen, which told him it was Donatella. He didn't feel like talking to his agent, so he ignored the call.

"I've got to go," he said, wiping his eyes. "I'm meeting Donatella about my next book."

"You've got another one coming out?" Brian asked, with a forced-looking smile. "I'm impressed."

"Donatella wants me to write a companion book to *Haunted California*, sort of my take on each episode. She says it'll be a cakewalk, but that sort of attitude scares the shit out of me."

"It'll be great. Everything you do is great."

They embraced again and agreed to remain friends. Before they parted ways, Blake promised he would continue to help Brian with unsolved cases at the SFPD. As Blake rode MUNI back toward downtown, however, he felt alone.

As he stood in the window looking at his spectacular view, he shook his head. Sex with the waiter had been a mistake. If anything, it made him feel even more alone. Why couldn't Brian have accepted him for who he was?

With a sigh, he turned off the lights in his beautiful, empty apartment and went to bed, pushing the bitter memories aside.

CHAPTER EIGHT

Melody Adams was sitting at her desk at Danzig Paranormal Investigations, reading a tarot spread. Technically, she was there to answer the phone and field any possible walk-ins, but since business had been unusually slow, she decided to practice the tarot. Since his breakup with Brian, Blake had taken some time off to work on his next book. Fortunately, there were no episodes to be taped for another month and, as usual, Melody had readily agreed to help out.

Melody stared at the cards in front of her and wrinkled her nose disapprovingly. She quickly consulted her tarot guide, a book she had bought downtown, and after a moment snapped it shut with a sigh. Clairvoyant or not, she doubted she would ever get the hang of card reading. There were simply too many rules, too many variables. And it didn't matter that the Death card really meant new beginnings—every time she drew the card it creeped her out. But born the youngest of three girls, Melody was anything but a quitter, having learned long ago that nothing in life ever came easy. Someone was always bigger or stronger, and, in order to get ahead, she would have to fight. She was reshuffling the cards when the bell above the door startled her. She looked up to see a heavy-set, middle-aged man cautiously enter.

He looked around nervously and cleared his throat before he spoke. "Is this the ghost place?"

Melody appraised the new arrival. His rough hands had what appeared to be motor oil under the nails, his faded jeans needed a good washing, and he looked as if he hadn't shaved in two days. The baseball cap on his head was an advertisement for a car-parts manufacturer. Melody sensed he was in great distress.

"Yes," she said, rising from her chair. "May I help you?"

The man hesitated and looked as if he wanted to bolt for the door.

"Is...is Mr. Danzig in?" he asked, having great difficulty meeting Melody's eyes.

"Mr. Danzig is working on a case out of the office," she lied. "I'm his assistant, Melody. Is there anything I can do to help you?"

"Do you see them, too?" His voice was nearly a whisper.

"In a sense," Melody replied, vaguely. "And I can sense that you're really quite distressed about something. Would you like to tell me about it?"

She gestured to a chair in front of the desk and the new arrival regarded it suspiciously before slowly sitting.

"See, I've got a garage...an auto-repair place over on Divisadero," he said, nervously, "and things happen there, especially at night."

"I see. What sort of things?"

"I don't know. Hell, things move around by themselves, doors open and close by themselves, weird noises. It's wearing me out."

"How long has this been going on?"

"Since I bought the place ten years ago, but it's been getting worse lately."

"How do you mean?"

"It's throwing things at me…in broad daylight!" the man shouted. "You think I made this up?" He removing his hat and pointed to a large red bump on his head.

"I understand that you're upset," she said, trying to calm the man. "We'll do everything we can to help you. Please write your address down here and maybe we can come by tomorrow, around two?"

As the man scrawled his address, he seemed to relax. "Two o'clock would be great," he said, "the sooner, the better!"

After he left she couldn't help but laugh. A couple of years earlier she would never have imagined herself working in paranormal investigations. It was certainly different from the downtown law office where she had been working—and not fitting in—before she quit, sick of the corporate world. And it was even further from her Southern Baptist upbringing back in her small Midwestern hometown, where everyone— her parents included—considered her an unholy freak because of her unusual "gifts." Even the other kids in her small school avoided her, nicknaming her "spooky girl." Her only friend was her mother's sister, Jane, an unmarried, childless woman, who treated Melody as if she was her own child. She suggested that Melody leave their small town as soon as she was old enough.

"I wish I'd gotten out of here when I was your age," Aunt Jane whispered conspiratorially.

And, although she wasn't sure, Melody had suspected that Aunt Jane was perhaps a lesbian, too, although back then Melody was many years away from discussing her sexuality with anyone. Unfortunately, Aunt Jane died from cancer when Melody was seventeen, leaving her alone in an unfriendly town, anxiously waiting to be old enough to leave.

On her eighteenth birthday, Melody said good-bye to her hometown and jumped the first bus to San Francisco to start a new life. After a series of disastrous jobs, including one at a law firm where she was forced to wear corporate drag and uncomfortable shoes and another at a coffee shop where she was overworked and underpaid, she had walked into Blake Danzig's storefront to inquire about a job ad she had seen in a newspaper. The volume of new clients had overwhelmed Blake, so he needed an assistant, and the two of them quickly hit it off. He hired Melody immediately, saying that he was especially impressed at Melody's lack of surprise when he informed her that an elderly, female ghost was following her.

"Oh, I know," she had replied calmly. "That's my aunt Jane. She came with me to California when I moved here to keep an eye on me."

Melody looked at the clock on the wall and remembered she was supposed to meet Blake at the Bayside Bar, a South of Market watering hole. She cursed and hurriedly began to gather her things.

Blake was seated at the bar of the Bayside Bar waiting for Melody. Just across the street was the restaurant where he had met the redheaded waiter, Darren, or whatever the hell his name was, the night before, and Blake tried once again to push away his loneliness since losing Brian. How many guys had he been with since the breakup? Fifteen…twenty? Blake couldn't recall but only knew that none of them wanted to hang around a guy who talked to ghosts—no longer than a fuck or two, anyway. He glanced at his watch. As usual, Melody was late. He took a sip of his beer and scanned the crowded room. The bar was dark, with its walls painted black and the only windows near the front of the bar. Those were tinted, so passersby couldn't see in. Why did so many gay bars choose to be so dark and dreary inside? Perhaps because so many gay men seemed to love an air of mystery?

Even though he was the star of a very popular show on the FX network, nobody seemed to have recognized him, and he was grateful. In fact, the only person paying Blake any attention—aside from the cute bartender—was a hot blond at the end of the bar. The kid was probably in his late twenties, a little young for his personal taste, but the kid's lean body and muscular biceps were enough to pique Blake's curiosity. Like with the redheaded waiter, Blake could see where this was heading.

The blond leered at Blake and rose from his bar stool, never removing his eyes from Blake.

Here it comes, Blake thought. *Either he's seen my show or wants me to fuck him or both.* Instead, the blond walked toward the bathrooms at the back of the bar, a signal that Blake interpreted as an invitation for bathroom sex. It wouldn't be the first time he'd been blown in a men's room, and at least he had a condom with him. He was still mulling over the invitation when the blond walked through the back wall and vanished. Blake sighed loudly, finished his beer, and ordered another.

This wasn't the first time Blake had seen a ghost in a bar. They were everywhere, and Blake had learned long ago never to speak to someone unless he had seen another living human speak to the stranger first. Blake realized this behavior, *especially* in a bar, might make him seem like an asshole to some, but it was necessary. Otherwise, he risked looking like a drunk or, worse, crazy, which had happened a year earlier in a bar in Pasadena. Blake had wandered in for a beer, only to find the place nearly empty. Aside from the bartender, the only people present were an older gay man, who nodded at Blake as he passed, and a dark-haired, fortyish man sitting near the far end of the bar. After he ordered the beer from the bartender, the dark-haired man spoke first. His name was Chad, he had explained, and he was very happy to see a new face in the bar. Blake had smiled, mistaking the stranger's banter for flirting. After twenty minutes of back-and-forth with the stranger, Blake was surprised by the bartender, who suddenly appeared in front of him, his arms crossed.

"I don't know what you're on, buddy," he had said, his eyes narrowed. "But you'd better go."

Blake stared dumbly at the bartender but, when he turned to his companion for help, he was shocked to see that he had vanished. Humiliated, he quickly paid the tab and retreated, under the accusing eyes of the bartender and his lone customer. It had been an embarrassing moment, but it had taught Blake two valuable lessons: First, ghosts are everywhere and sometimes they look like real, living people. Second, he needed to use caution when speaking to anyone in public. Otherwise he risked ridicule and, possibly, the loony bin. Still, the blond who had just walked through the wall intrigued Blake and, since he was still waiting for Melody, he caught the cute bartender's attention.

"What's up?" he asked in a friendly manner. "Your drink okay?"

"Yeah." Blake looked from side to side to make sure nobody was eavesdropping. "Have you ever felt anything here…anything creepy?"

The bartender chuckled. "You mean like ghosts?"

"Yeah. It wouldn't be unusual for a place like this to be haunted."

"Sorry," the bartender said, then laughed, "but I don't believe in ghosts. Now, the owner, he's a different story…says things move around in the office." He gestured back toward the restrooms.

"The office is back by the restrooms?"

"On the other side of the wall. The owner calls the ghost Charlie."

"Why Charlie?"

"Who the hell knows? Probably too many drugs in the seventies. Excuse me," he said as two men approached the bar at the other end.

Just then Melody walked in the door looking harried. Blake waved at her from his seat and she joined him. "You're late," he teased her.

Blake chuckled at the words as soon as they escaped his lips. Melody was always late, and it had become an ongoing joke between them. Blake suspected, in fact, that Melody would one day be late to her own funeral. Had Melody been early, now *that* would have been a true surprise.

"Sorry," she said, "it was murder getting a cab."

"How was work?"

"Mostly dead, no pun intended. But a guy named Jake came in late in the day…says he's got a haunted business space over on Divisadero."

"Do you think he does?" Blake took a sip of his beer.

"He had a knot on his head he says the ghost caused."

"A poltergeist? Did you schedule him?"

"Tomorrow afternoon. How's the book going?"

"Okay, I suppose."

"What's wrong?"

"I don't know. I guess I'm not that into it. I mean, it's just a rehash of some of the more interesting episodes of the show from my personal perspective."

"So that should be easy." Melody waved for the bartender's attention. "You always keep good notes. Just work from those."

The bartender appeared in front of them and Melody ordered a beer.

"Maybe that's the problem," Blake said, once the bartender had gone. "Maybe it's too easy and that scares me."

"You worry too much."

The bartender came back and placed the beer in front of Melody. "You know what you were saying earlier?" he asked Blake.

Blake nodded.

"I guess I never thought about it until now, but I have noticed strange things, like glasses moving or the jukebox coming on for no particular reason."

Melody looked at Blake, clueless. Blake quickly explained and turned back to the bartender. "And you don't think those things are odd?"

The bartender shook his head. "A big truck driving past could make glasses move," he shrugged, "or an earthquake. As for the jukebox, well, electronics fuck up all the time."

It amazed Blake how many people simply refused to believe in spirits, despite the mountains of evidence right in front of them. Then again, maybe he was wrong. Maybe the spirits fed off the energy of the believers of the world in order to gain the strength they needed to appear. As soon as the bartender had excused himself to serve yet more customers, Blake turned back to Melody.

"Clueless," he said, though not unkindly.

"Most people are."

"Listen," he said, changing the subject, "I'm thinking of taking a trip to New Mexico to see my parents. Maybe I can work on the book while I'm down there."

"Okay. When are you going?"

"Friday. Maybe I'll stay down there a week or so."

"Friday? This Friday? That's day after tomorrow."

"I know." Blake laughed. "We'll take care of the Divisadero poltergeist tomorrow, then close for a week. Unless you want to work while I'm gone."

"Danzig Paranormal Investigations isn't much without you. I'm just a clairvoyant. I can't get rid of ghosts."

"You're a very valuable part of what we do. Take the week off, then. I'll consider it vacation."

The next day Blake and Melody met Jake at his auto-repair shop on Divisadero. From the outside, the single-story white stucco building looked like any other garage. Once inside, however, it was as if alarms were going off inside Melody's head. To make matters worse, the temperature seemed to have dropped considerably.

"I don't like this, Blake." Melody's breath was visible in the chilly air.

Suddenly, the overhead lights began to flicker.

"He's here," Jake whispered, looking terrified.

"You wait outside." Blake pointed the terrified owner out to the sidewalk. "You don't need to be here."

A hubcap careened through the air, nearly striking Jake in the head. Without further prompting he ran for the door.

Suddenly, from the darkness that was the back of the garage came a low animal growl.

"Get out!" screeched a voice that sounded like a hundred voices in unison.

"Who are you?" Blake demanded. "Show yourself!"

The shadows at the back of the garage began to converge into one spot, thickening until they made up one single form.

"Blake," Melody said, terror in her eyes, "this isn't a ghost. This thing was conjured by dark magic."

Melody did her best to hide her fear, not wanting to give the entity negative energy on which to feed. But that someone, possibly inexperienced teenagers, had toyed with the Craft as if it were a game and unleashed a dangerous demon infuriated her. How would witches ever gain respect when so many kids recklessly cast spells they found all too easily in books and on the Internet?

"What the hell is it?" Blake asked.

Before she could elaborate, unseen forces picked Blake up and tossed him like a rag doll against the far wall. He fell to the floor and the dark mist advanced upon him.

"Stop," Melody bellowed.

The entity stopped and drifted toward Melody, hovering in front of her.

"Who summoned you?" she demanded.

Although she was terrified, Melody refused to show it. To do so would most definitely mean defeat and, worse, possible possession by the entity. An amateur witch had probably conjured this thing—a demon—and not properly released it. With luck, perhaps she could.

"Witch," the black form hissed.

"I release you back to your realm," she said, and stretched out her arms. "Go now. Leave this place and cause no more harm. I command you!"

The entity did not respond, merely cackled a low, gurgling laugh, a laugh that sent shivers down Melody's spine.

"You did not summon me," the entity replied, "and you have no power to banish me."

Melody pulled a dagger from under her skirt and the prop shocked even Blake, who stared at her with disbelieving eyes. Melody raised the dagger and drew a banishing pentagram in the air, her eyes tightly closed.

"By the powers of the Guardians of the Four Watchtowers, I banish you," she chanted. "Return to your realm now!"

The entity hissed in response, but Melody repeated her words once more.

Blake, who was still trying to shake himself from the stupor caused by being slammed against the wall and by the sudden appearance of the dagger, was amazed to see the dark cloud shrink, then disappear altogether, the hundreds of voices slowly falling silent. Almost immediately the temperature began to rise in the garage. Blake pulled himself up from the floor and approached Melody, who was as amazed as he was that her trick had worked.

"Not a poltergeist?" He cradled his injured arm.

"No," a grin slowly crept across her face, "a demon."

"Where the hell did you get that dagger?"

"It's my athame." Melody tucked it back under her skirt. "A good witch never leaves home without hers."

Blake put his arm around Melody and squeezed her shoulder. "Who says Danzig Paranormal only works when I'm around?"

Together they walked out onto the sunny street in search of Jake to tell him the good news.

CHAPTER NINE

Friday morning was gray, with no hint of blue sky. It was one of those San Francisco days that was neither sunny nor rainy, and Blake was happy to be headed for a warmer climate, if only for a week. He arrived at the gate, single carry-on in tow, just as the first call for boarding was announced. As he waited in line with his fellow passengers, Blake became aware of a familiar voice nearby. He craned his neck to find the source, somewhere in front of him, and was mortified to spy none other than Clive Damon, his British counterpart.

Clive Damon was host of the televised show *Haunted Isle*, which each week investigated supposed hauntings at various castles, inns, and cemeteries all over the U.K. Blake loathed the show and its treatment of the paranormal, even though he watched it faithfully, if only to compare notes for his own show. He hated *Haunted Isle* first because the show's producers insisted upon filming in night vision, which, in Blake's opinion, was merely a cheap way to heighten the suspense and basically force its viewers to be frightened. Second, Clive's co-stars were prone to hysterics; any sound, real or imagined, was made virtually indecipherable in the recordings, drowned out by their frenzied screams of terror. But, most maddening,

Clive Damon was an absolute fraud, who could no more talk to ghosts than he could Martians. Unfortunately, Clive was quite handsome, standing at an impressive six-one with straw-blond hair and piercing blue eyes. Even at the age of forty, he had a porcelain complexion. He looked like royalty, in a linen suit and silk tie, and he played his role to the hilt. While Blake hated to admit it, Clive was hot. Not Blake's type, but still hot.

Blake had met Clive once, during a stop on a book tour in New York, and though they were technically rivals, the meeting had been cordial. Blake silently prayed the Brit wouldn't notice him. Otherwise, he would be forced to listen to Clive talk about how wonderful his own show was during the entire flight.

However, Clive was seated in the same row, just on the other side of the aisle. Blake's heart sank when he realized his misfortune and he tried, unsuccessfully, to squeeze past his seatmate, a young, blond female in her thirties, before Clive could see him.

"Danzig?" Clive drawled. "Is that Blake Danzig?"

His face red, Blake busied himself stowing his bag in the overhead compartment "Hello, Clive," he said graciously. "What a coincidence."

"Isn't it?" Clive grasped Blake's hand firmly.

Blake sat down in his seat and nodded at the blonde, wishing for nothing more than silence for the rest of the flight. However, Clive leaned over and continued talking.

"What sends you to New Mexico, old boy?" He flashed his dazzling smile.

"My parents retired there, near Albuquerque. I'm just going down to visit them for a week."

"Marvelous, simply marvelous."

"How about you? What brings you to America's Southwest?"

"I'm meeting with some gentlemen from the New Mexico Ghost Hunters' Investigations in Albuquerque. I've watched their show and was quite impressed."

The young woman seated on the aisle looked at Clive. "Would you like to trade seats?"

Blake was about to politely decline her offer but Clive cut him off.

"That would be most kind of you," he said, rising from his seat as he spoke, "very kind, indeed."

The blonde turned to Blake as she gathered her bag from under the seat in front of her.

"I really like your show," she whispered.

This kindness—the fact she had recognized him yet not made a huge scene—made Blake soften a bit. He thanked her as she moved across the aisle to Clive's seat and Clive settled into her recently vacated spot. Blake sighed and couldn't help but notice the faint, sweet scent of Clive's cologne, vetiver, perhaps.

"I saw your show on Mary, Queen of Scots," Blake said. "It was fascinating."

"Thank you. I believe it was one of our best so far."

Blake wanted to add that it was a pity that no actual images or recordings were captured and that Clive had presented "a feeling" as the only "proof" of the ghost's existence, but he held his tongue.

"I saw the bit your people did on the Winchester Mystery House. Smashing…absolutely smashing!"

"Thank you. We just taped a segment at the Hollywood Roosevelt Hotel in LA, which will air on Halloween."

"Wonderful. And the Roosevelt—is it quite haunted?"

"Quite. Marilyn Monroe still inhabits the place."

"Fascinating." Clive leaned close and whispered, conspiratorially, "You must see what we've put together for All Hallows Eve."

"What is it?"

Clive looked from side to side to make sure no one was eavesdropping. "The ghost of William Shakespeare at an inn at Stratford upon Avon!"

"Really?" Blake was unable to resist a slight dig. "And you managed to capture him on camera?"

"You'll be surprised," Clive replied, nonchalantly, though Blake could tell from his expression he had struck a nerve.

❖

As the passengers prepared to exit the plane at Albuquerque International Sunport, Clive hastily jotted down the name of his hotel in Albuquerque and insisted Blake visit him while he was in town.

"I'll try," Blake lied, "but I'm sure I'll be very busy with my parents."

"Just one drink. Besides, you might want to come with me to meet these ghost-hunter chaps."

Blake tucked the piece of paper into the back pocket of his jeans and nodded. Meeting other ghost hunters, while often disappointing, was never a bad idea. Sometimes he learned something.

"I'll give you a call," he said, and they shook hands before parting in the busy terminal. Out on the sidewalk, Blake waited in line for a taxi. The air was warm and dry, and though it was a pleasant change from the weather in chilly San Francisco, sweat quickly appeared under the arms of Blake's light gray

T-shirt. Finally it was his turn in line, and Blake quickly got in the next taxi. He gave the driver, an older Latino man in his late forties, the address of his parents' house in nearby Pajarito.

As they sped away from the airport and got on the highway, the driver made small talk about his family and the weather, two safe topics for engaging strangers. They passed through the small suburbs of Atrisco, Los Padillas, Kinney, and Mountain View on the way, magnificent mountains looming in the foreground. Once in Pajarito, an area known locally as the south valley and traditionally farmland, Blake marveled at all the new construction.

"Always more new subdivisions," the cab driver lamented. "Soon there will be no land left for agriculture."

Before the cab driver even stopped the car, Blake recognized his parents' house, though he had never been there. The house, which Blake surmised was built sometime in the thirties, was painted in garish pink and purple tones, and hundreds of wind chimes hung from the trees in the front yard. Although they had retired from the circus, apparently his parents would always be circus people deep inside. Blake paid the fare and thanked the driver before getting out. As he approached the house by way of a winding sidewalk, his mother appeared in the doorway. She was in her sixties, and her long brown hair had turned white, but she still had the same youthful glow and sparkling brown eyes.

She threw open the screen door and hugged him. "Blake, it's so good to see you."

She led him into the house, the interior as eclectic as its exterior, and into the living room. Small crystals hung in every window and, on a table under a window, a tarot spread lay open next to a crystal ball. A black cat, named Dexter, rested on the sill. Beads and bells hung in every doorway. Myriad pillows in every pattern imaginable were scattered across the floor, tossed onto thick Oriental rugs, and books, some very old and valuable, were stacked in a corner of the room. It was as if his parents had robbed a gypsy caravan.

"How was your flight?" She touched Blake's cheek. "Are you hungry?"

"The flight was okay," Blake said, placing his bag on the floor. "I had the misfortune of sitting next to Clive Damon the entire time, though."

Lila Danzig's face screwed up into a scowl. "That awful British fraud? Your show is so much better than his."

"I know, but thank you for saying so."

"Your father and I never miss your show," she said, beaming. "We're so proud of you."

"Where is Dad?" Blake was embarrassed by the flattery.

"In the backyard." Lila waved toward the back of the house. "These days his little vegetable garden is about all he has time for."

Just then a young girl in a ruffled white dress skipped through an interior wall, across the living room, then through the wall leading to the side yard before disappearing.

"Um, Mom, do you know you have the ghost of a little girl here?"

"Of course." Lila laughed. "Her name is Jacqueline and she used to live in the house next door. I contacted her during a séance. Things kept disappearing around the house, so we were suspicious. But she's a harmless little thing."

Blake mused at his mother's nonchalance. Why couldn't Brian have accepted the existence of spirits so easily? Then again, Blake reminded himself, his family was anything but normal, so why did he assume everyone he met could so easily accept him?

"You'll see lots of ghosts while you're here," Lila said. "I believe it's because of the ley lines."

Blake nodded, but hesitated to respond. Even though he was far from being a skeptic when it came to the supernatural, the theory of ley lines—supposed invisible, mystical lines that ran under the ground—was something he had no opinion about.

"Let's go find your father." Lila led him into a bright, yellow kitchen and to a screened back door leading out into the garden.

As she had predicted, Ben Danzig was on his knees fighting with a bamboo stake, meant to support a pea plant. Blake marveled at the mini-oasis stretched out before him. His parents had obviously put a lot of effort into the small space allotted to them. Various plants and wildflowers filled the walled garden. It was crowned by a koi pond, placed against the back wall and fed by a gurgling fountain. Blake almost forgot he was in the desert and wondered how his father had coaxed so many species of flowers and plants to grow in the arid soil. The bright orange koi moved smoothly just beneath the surface of the clear water, their languid movements almost hypnotically soothing.

His father turned at the approach of visitors and his face lit up.

"Hi, Dad," Blake said.

Just like his mother, his father had aged considerably, and white hair poked out from under his straw hat. The stoop of Ben Danzig's shoulders contrasted to his otherwise healthy appearance, his still-thin body in excellent shape from his years as a contortionist.

He struggled to his feet and hugged Blake warmly. "When did you get here?"

"Just a few minutes ago. How've you been, Dad?"

"Good, good." Ben gestured to the garden behind him. "If only I could keep the rabbits out of my vegetables!"

"It's a nice garden," Blake said. "You can't really blame them."

"How's Brian?" Although Ben had no problem with homosexuals, he had always been slightly disappointed with the knowledge he would never have grandchildren. Still, his love for his son was strong and—grandchildren or not—he was determined to be supportive.

"Brian and I broke up."

"What happened?" Lila looked concerned. "I thought things were going well."

"It's a long story." Blake was in no mood to relive the breakup. "Can we talk about it later?"

"Of course. Why don't we all go in and eat a little lunch? I've got leftover lasagna I can heat up, and we'll open a nice bottle of wine."

"Sounds excellent." Blake suddenly realized he was, indeed, hungry.

Lila placed her arm around his waist and led him back into the house, with Ben following closely behind.

CHAPTER TEN

For the first few days at his parents' house, Blake felt more relaxed than he had in a long while. He slept late, watched television with his parents, and read in the garden while his father tended to his vegetables. More importantly, he was finally beginning to make progress on his manuscript for the new book, the peace and quiet of his parents' house apparently the stimulus he needed. For Blake, it was a welcome change to allow himself to be taken care of, and his parents were all too happy to indulge him. Lila cooked more than she had in years, making Blake the most elaborate of meals and causing Ben to wisecrack to his son that he needed to visit more often, if only to inspire Lila to cook.

Ignoring her husband's joke, she turned to Blake, her face serious. "You really should come and visit more often," she said, in a way only a mother could. "Perhaps you could come back in October for the balloon festival."

Ben explained to Blake that in October, Albuquerque hosted the International Balloon Fiesta, one of the largest gatherings of hot-air balloons in the world.

"It's quite something to see, hundreds and hundreds of hot-air balloons of every color imaginable in the sky."

"It sounds great. I'll have to look at my calendar and see if I've got anything going on, but—"

"No pressure," Ben said. "Your mother is just trying to say we wouldn't mind seeing a little more of you."

Just then, Blake's cell phone rang. Grateful for the momentary reprieve from the well-intentioned lecture he felt coming, he looked at the familiar number displayed on the phone's screen. Melody had decided at the last minute to man the office in Blake's absence. As a concession, she agreed to take the week off after Blake returned.

"It's Melody," he said. "I should take this in case she needs something."

"Tell her we said hello," Lila called as Blake stepped out into the garden.

"Hey," Blake said, once he was outside, "how are things in San Francisco?"

"Fine. It's been quiet here. How are the parents?"

"They're fine, but I was just getting the 'you need to come and visit more often' talk when you called."

"Ouch." Melody laughed. "Nobody likes to be reminded of what a negligent child they've been."

"Tell me about it. They mean well, but I'm going to try to get out of the house today. Maybe do a little sightseeing."

"How's the manuscript?"

"It's coming along nicely. You were right, of course. I was making it more difficult than it really was. But I think the change of scenery has been good for me, and for the book."

"That's great, Blake. Well, I should let you go. I just wanted to check in. When are you coming back to San Francisco?"

"I'm flying back this weekend, on Saturday. I'll call you when I get in."

He hung up and went back in the house, where his parents were still seated at the small kitchen table.

"If you guys don't mind," he said, "I'm going into town today to do a little looking around."

"Of course not, dear," Lila replied. "Will you be home for dinner?"

"Yes, Mom." Blake kissed her on the forehead. "I don't plan to stay out all night and paint the town red."

"Well, you never know who you might meet," Lila said.

Blake ignored his mother's comment and went up to the spare room that he was using. He slipped off his khaki shorts and picked up his jeans, which he had tossed over the back of a nearby chair. As he did so, a piece of paper fell from the back pocket onto the hardwood floor. It was the telephone number to Clive Damon's hotel. Impulsively, he dialed the number and the front-desk clerk connected him to Clive's room. The familiar voice answered on the third ring.

"Blake," he said cheerfully. "I was beginning to think you had forgotten that I was in town. But here you are, and just in time."

"What do you mean?"

"I'm meeting with the paranormal chaps this afternoon. You must accompany me."

"Sure." As long as he had to endure Clive Damon's company, he was happy he could perhaps make it worthwhile. "Where should I meet you?"

"Take a taxi to my hotel, and we'll go there together."

Blake agreed and hung up. Downstairs, Lila called a taxi and, ten minutes later, Blake was headed toward Albuquerque's Old Town.

Normally, given his unique predilection for seeing

ghosts, he would have been apprehensive about going to a place called Old Town. But, relieved to feel a sense of independence, Blake decided not to worry about it. He arrived at Clive's hotel before he knew it. As he had suspected, the area was crawling with ghosts. Men and women wandered the streets in turn-of-the-century Western gear, the spirits of Native Americans walked the streets leading horses, and the occasional 1940s-era soldier passed by on the sidewalk. Fortunately Clive was waiting in front of the hotel as they pulled up. He waved and joined Blake in the backseat, then gave the address of their destination to the driver. The driver thought for a moment, then turned to them.

"I don't mind driving you there," he said, "but that's just a block up, around the next corner."

"I don't mind walking, if you don't," Blake said, looking at Clive.

"It's just that it's so hot." Clive had a pained expression on his face.

"Suit yourself," the cabbie replied. "It's your dime."

True to his word, at the end of the block, the driver turned right onto the next street and stopped in front of a two-story building in the middle of the block. Unlike the majority of the adobe-style buildings in Old Town, the building was wooden and looked straight out of an old Western, complete with swinging doors. And although the street was paved, there were hitching posts in front for horses. Blake paid the fare and they emerged from the cab and out onto the sidewalk, where the spirit of a saloon girl passed right through Clive's body. Not surprisingly, his face registered no knowledge of this having happened, strengthening Blake's conviction that his peer was nothing more than a charlatan.

"Shall we?" Clive led the way up onto the wooden porch of the building and through the swinging doors. A large man, who Blake recognized as Hank Duffy, the host and creator of the New Mexico Ghost Hunters' Investigations show, approached as they entered. He wore a cowboy hat and was built like a linebacker, but he greeted them warmly.

"I'll be damned." He grasped Clive's hand and pumped his arm as if he was trying to obtain water. "Mr. Damon, it's a real honor to meet you! I'm a real big fan of your show."

"Thank you." Clive flexed his hand as if it ached. "May I also present Blake Danzig?"

"This is a real treat." Hank gave Blake's outstretched hand the same treatment he had given Clive's. "How do you do, Mr. Danzig? Of course, I'm a real big fan of your show, too."

Hank Duffy, an affable man in his mid-fifties, had founded the New Mexico Ghost Hunters' Investigations thirty years earlier with his brother, Dan, and was the author of numerous books on the subject of ghosts. What impressed Blake most about Hank was that he initially treated his investigations with obvious skepticism, first viewing possible "hauntings" with a scientific eye. To Blake, this approach lent credence to the organization. Unfortunately, it also caused feelings of resentment from those who truly believed they were being haunted. Nevertheless, Hank Duffy was well-respected in the paranormal community for his guarded approach to the supernatural.

He led his guests to a large round wooden table in the middle of the room. The massive room seemed to have been torn directly from the Old West. Massive wooden beams on the ceiling ran from wall to wall, and the wooden floor planks were wide and rough-hewn, as if made by hand at a local sawmill. The wooden walls, too, were rough and covered haphazardly with whitewash, dotted here and there with old Western photographs. Thick rugs with ornate Native American designs were thrown on the floor in various spaces, and an old upright piano stood in a far corner. Blake found himself momentarily lost in a cowboy fantasy before he snapped back to the present and his companions.

A nearby wall was covered with more framed photos, these of orbs, shadows, and strange light anomalies. Blake guessed these were probably taken during previous investigations.

"So, Mr. Danzig," Hank said, "I was expecting Mr. Damon, but you're quite a surprise. What brings you to Albuquerque?"

"I'm here visiting my parents. I just happened to run into Clive on the flight down here and decided to tag along."

"As I told you in my letter," Clive said, clearly in no mood to be overshadowed by the younger ghost hunter, "I would like to accompany you to some known haunts here to get a feel for the locale and maybe put together a tape of my own show, sort of a U.K. visits the Old West."

"That's fine by me," Hank replied good-naturedly. "It puts me in good company."

Hank turned back to Blake. "And how about you, Mr. Danzig? Would you like to come along? We have plenty of hauntings in this area. I figured we could drive over to Los Lunas and Corrales tomorrow to start. They've each got some places that we found a lot of activity in. And we have quite a few spots right here in Albuquerque I can show you."

"Thank you, but I should really spend time with my parents before I return to San Francisco this weekend."

Hank thought for a moment, clearly disappointed. "Tell

you what. There's a place within walking distance from here that I could show you. You got time for that?"

"Sure. I'd love to."

Their destination, a café located in a centuries-old adobe structure, was haunted by its former resident. The café, whose walls were a rough adobe texture and held yet more framed black-and-white period photos, was small and cozy. High-backed chairs, shellacked a shiny black, were placed around the smattering of small tables and, to Blake, it seemed more Latin in flavor than Southwestern. The smell of food, which emanated from a kitchen in the back, made Blake's stomach growl, and he hoped no one else had noticed.

Blake spotted the café's ghost almost immediately, after he and Clive had both been introduced to the café's owner. He conveyed this information to his companions.

"I, too, sense a spirit," Clive proclaimed.

Blake resisted the urge to roll his eyes and was grateful when the owner spoke. "That's right," she said. "Staff and customers alike have seen our former resident. I think she really just likes to keep a watch over the place."

"She says she approves of what you are doing here," Blake said, repeating what the ghost told him.

"Amazing," Clive whispered.

Out on the street, their tour of the haunted café over, Clive agreed to meet Hank the following morning at the office of New Mexico Ghost Hunters' Investigations for their drive out of town. Hank shook hands with them both and disappeared down the sunny street.

"What do you say we have a drink?" Clive asked.

Blake looked at his watch. "I should probably get back to my parents' house." Unfortunately, no taxis were in sight.

"Come on," Clive said. "We'll have a drink back at the hotel. Besides, it will be much easier to get a taxi from there."

Blake realized Clive was right, so together they walked to Clive's hotel. By the time they got there, however, Clive was sweating profusely.

"Let's go to my room," he said, "so I can freshen up."

He led Blake through an adobe-walled archway and into a lushly planted courtyard. They passed numerous units, in front of which sat patio furniture, brightly colored lamps, and gurgling fountains, and finally arrived at Clive's quarters.

"I'll wait out here." Blake said, tugging at a patio chair.

Clive opened his door. "Nonsense. Come inside where it's cool. Besides, you simply must see this place."

Blake reluctantly followed him through the door. The interior of the unit was spacious, with adobe walls, a fireplace in one corner, and large rustic furniture. Blake noticed a hot tub in an alcove. "Nice," he said as Clive disappeared into the bathroom.

He could hear water running in the other room and was just about to take a seat in a large, overstuffed chair covered in a Southwestern-style fabric, when Clive called from the bathroom.

"There's a complimentary bottle of wine on the table. Why don't you open it?"

Blake found the bottle, with a bottle opener conveniently located nearby, and uncorked it. He was filling two stemmed wineglasses when Clive emerged from the bathroom, wearing nothing but a robe.

"Clive, I can wait outside while you dress."

"Nonsense." He took a glass of wine from Blake and sat in the large chair. "Sit. Let's relax for a moment."

Blake hesitantly perched on the edge of the bed since Clive had taken the chair, and he took a sip of the peppery-tasting wine. Hating himself for the thought, Blake had to admit that Clive Damon had nice legs.

"You and I should consider teaming up," Clive said.

"What do you mean?"

"Just what I said, dear boy."

"What are you suggesting?"

"I don't know exactly. It's just a thought. You and I could be good together."

Clive draped a leg over the arm of the chair, which opened the front of his robe, revealing a fat, uncut cock.

Blake struggled for words. "Clive." He couldn't look away from the growing erection. "I don't think this is a good idea."

Clive placed his glass of wine on the small table beside the chair and stood up, dropping the robe as he did so. At that point he was rock-hard, and he approached the bed. Blake was surprised at the extraordinary condition of Clive's smooth, muscular body. Despite his reservations, his own cock was swelling in his tight jeans.

"Clive…"

Clive took the wineglass from Blake's hand and placed it beside his own on the bedside table. "Don't you fancy me?"

"Of course, but—"

Clive kissed him on the mouth and was tugging at the buttons on his jeans. Blake's face flushed as his resistance crumbled. Sure, Clive Damon was a pompous fraud, but he was incredibly handsome and built like a god. And that dick… He took Clive's tongue into his mouth and put his arms around him.

Clive pulled off Blake's T-shirt, then his jeans, revealing

his throbbing erection. "Very nice," he said. "I see that you do fancy me, after all."

Blake felt mildly humiliated, betrayed by his erect cock. Oddly, however, the humiliation turned him on, and he suddenly only wanted to be used.

"I do," he said. "I do fancy you. Do you want to fuck me, Clive?"

Without hesitation, Clive rolled Blake over onto his stomach, spat on his hand, and inserted a wet finger into Blake's asshole.

Blake sighed and arched his back, giving Clive greater access. Clive worked the warm asshole, inserting more fingers. Blake, who usually played the top in sexual encounters, groaned at the sensation of having his ass played with.

Clive quickly retrieved a condom and a tube of lubricant from a bag. "Are you ready? I want to devour your sweet ass."

"Give it to me, please," Blake whispered.

Clive, ever the gentleman, slowly pushed his uncut cock into Blake's tight hole.

Blake felt so dirty for what he was doing, something he knew was wrong, but his shame propelled him forward, riding Clive's dick with a passion. "Fuck me," he yelled. "Use that tight asshole."

Clive quickly came, shooting his load in Blake's ass.

Blake stroked off his own meat and forced Clive to keep his dick inside him as he did so.

"Fuck," he groaned, shooting his load across Clive's Southwestern-print bedspread.

❖

Blake had horribly degraded himself. Not that he hadn't enjoyed the sex or that Clive hadn't looked as good out of his clothes as Blake had imagined. Blake had allowed himself to be fucked by someone he truly despised. And he had enjoyed it. He quickly dressed and politely declined Clive's offer of another drink. As he departed, he promised to consider Clive's vague proposal and headed to the front of the hotel, searching for a cab. Once he had given his parents' address to the driver and settled in, he couldn't help but smile. What had he just done? If anyone had ever suggested such a pairing to him, he would have laughed. So why had he enjoyed sex with Clive Damon so much? As he headed towards his parents' house, Blake again felt very alone.

CHAPTER ELEVEN

B efore Blake knew it the week was over and he was once more telling his parents good-bye. Given his mother's obvious dislike for Clive, Blake had decided not to tell them he had spent time with him while in Albuquerque. Besides, Blake still wasn't sure what to make of what he had done. Sure, he had slept with lots of guys, especially since breaking up with Brian, but sex with Clive Damon had almost felt degrading, worse than being called a fraud by the redheaded waiter. Blake found the feeling oddly exhilarating, somewhere between filthy and titillated. If he couldn't figure it out, he sure as hell wouldn't mention it to his parents, even minus the sex. He did, however, tell them about all of the spirits he had seen in Old Town, a phenomenon his mother once again attributed to the ley lines.

With the first draft of his manuscript completed, Blake promised his parents he would seriously consider a return visit in the fall, something that seemed to greatly please them. After a quick ride to the airport, Blake boarded the plane and approached his seat, but spied a plump, fortyish redheaded woman seated in his assigned spot. He quickly checked his boarding pass to confirm his seat number and was about to ask the woman if she had the correct seat when she vanished.

Blake sighed and took the recently vacated seat. It was the first time, to the best of his knowledge, he had ever seen a ghost on an airplane. It made sense, though. Maybe the poor spirit had died of a heart attack on a previous flight. Maybe she had been a flight attendant on the plane. Whatever the circumstances, Blake was grateful that she had vanished before he had struck up a conversation with her. Nobody, after all, wanted to be stuck on a flight with a lunatic, and Blake certainly had no desire to be detained by airport security.

Fortunately, San Francisco was sunny and warm when Blake returned. As he vacated his cab, he realized that he was happy to be home. The buildings atop Nob Hill seemed to reflect the brilliant sunlight, and tourists milled about in front of the nearby Fairmont Hotel and in the park across the street. Inside his building, Blake was greeted by Mike, the affable doorman, who welcomed him back.

"How was New Mexico, Mr. Danzig?" he asked.

Although he had asked Mike on numerous occasions to address him by his first name, Mike simply refused to do so. Blake supposed that it was a matter of personal ethics for the doorman, as if deviating from his training was tantamount to failure, and Blake had stopped pushing him long ago.

"New Mexico is beautiful. But it's really good to be home."

"It's always nice to come home after being away on a trip, sir."

He pressed the button to call the elevator and, once Blake was inside with his bag, bade him good day. The door was just about to close when Mike, remembering something, stuck his hand inside the doors, staying them.

"I almost forgot, Mr. Danzig," he said, apologetically. "A

young guy was here to see you while you were gone. I told him you were out of town, but I saw him hanging around across the street a couple of days later, like he was waiting for you."

Blake frowned and stepped back out of the elevator. "What was his name?"

Mike shook his head. "That's the weird thing," he said. "He didn't tell me his name. I asked but, instead of answering, he turned and walked out the door."

"What did he look like?"

"Average height, blond, probably in his twenties."

Blake ran through a mental list of everyone he'd met over the course of previous months, but nobody came to mind.

"I didn't call the police," Mike said, "in case it was somebody legit. But, if you want me to, I'll take care of it."

Blake slowly shook his head. Could he have a stalker? "No, don't worry about it. I'm sure it's fine."

He thanked Mike and reboarded the elevator. Upstairs, in his apartment, thoughts of the mysterious visitor plagued Blake. Certain it was nothing to be concerned with, he pressed the replay button on his answering machine, which announced that he had two new messages. The first was from Donatella.

"Welcome home," she said. "Meet me in North Beach tomorrow for brunch. Make it eleven o'clock, at Caffe Roma. I can't wait to see what you've written. Ciao."

Blake chuckled. Donatella's messages were always to the point. The next message was from Brian. The sound of the familiar voice instantly filled Blake with melancholy, and his heart ached with yearning and bittersweet nostalgia.

"Hi, Blake," he said. "Melody said you were in Albuquerque visiting your parents, so I didn't want to call your cell phone and risk bothering you. Listen, when you get back give me a call. There's a case I think that you can help us with." There was a pause. "I miss you."

Brian's final statement cheered Blake a little. At least, he told himself, the feelings surrounding their breakup seemed to be mutual. Still, he decided to wait and call Brian on Monday. After all, he was still attempting to process what had happened between him and Clive, and seeing Brian certainly wouldn't do anything to help clarify the way he was feeling. Was he even the same person? Or had he crossed some sort of invisible bridge, one that took him to a different sexual level, one on which he allowed himself to be used by other men with no regard for the possibility of a real relationship?

As much as he hated to admit it, even to himself, Blake wanted to be with Clive again, if only to feel what he had in Albuquerque. Even the humiliation of fucking Clive Damon had provided Blake with the feelings he so desperately longed for, an attachment in some way to another man. He shrugged off the notion and quickly dialed Melody's number.

"You're back," she said, by way of answering.

"Just a few minutes ago. Anything going on I should know about?"

"Brian called. He said something about a case."

"I know. He left a message on my machine. Did anybody else call?"

"Hmm. Nobody important, why?"

"Did anybody come by looking for me? My doorman, Mike, said a guy was hanging around the building."

"No, nobody." Melody laughed. "Think you've got a crazed fan stalking you?"

"Not funny, although the thought did occur to me."

"Listen, if Brian has a new case I can wait and take another week off."

"No, enjoy some time off. I'm sure I can handle whatever Brian has for us. Besides," he added, teasingly, "when was the last time you got laid?"

"What year is it?" Melody deadpanned.

Although Melody knew Blake was joking, she seemed to be immune to long-term relationships. Her last girlfriend had been hot enough and was certainly interesting. Unfortunately, she had never been quite comfortable with the whole witchcraft thing, an attitude that Melody had found quite puzzling coming from a dominant butch lesbian into S&M. And she wasn't alone. Another one, so into her space as an alternative lesbian painter, might as well have been a Baptist minister by the way she reacted when she learned Melody was a witch. Even a lesbian performance-artist extraordinaire had run screaming for the hills. Where the hell were all the lesbian goddess worshippers, anyway?

Nevertheless, Melody had never run from a challenge, and she planned to do a little barhopping during her week off. She wished Blake a good night and made him promise to call her if he needed anything.

Her cat, Pyewackket, rubbed against her legs and she picked up the sleek Siamese male.

"Want to help Mama find her soul mate?" she asked, stroking the cat's head.

Pyewackket, whose whiskers were fanned out, purred in reply.

Melody walked to the small table she used as her altar and put Pyewackket on the floor. From a drawer in the table she retrieved a map of the city, which she folded in such a way that only a section of the Mission District, her neighborhood, was visible. Because it was also home to most of the city's lesbian bars, the Mission was the focus of her magic, and she pulled a crystal attached to a small length of silver chain from the drawer.

"Now, help Mama concentrate," she said to her cat, who was watching her with his big blue eyes. "Which bar will be the one tonight?"

As she concentrated, not on a particular bar or even a particular person, the crystal began to slowly rotate above the map, moved by unseen forces. Melody ignored the clockwise spinning and focused, instead, on what she imagined to be the perfect partner: a professional, slightly older than her, a nice body, blond, maybe. And she would definitely not be afraid of witchcraft.

The sound of the crystal making sudden contact with the table top caused Melody to open her eyes, and she cautiously consulted the map. She considered the location indicated by the crystal, furrowing her brow as she contemplated the location. She laughed, suddenly recognizing the intersection and the bar located there.

"Looks like it's the Kitty Kat Lounge tonight," she announced to Pyewackket. "At least I can walk there."

Pyewackket meowed his approval and Melody replaced the map and the crystal pendant in the drawer. She then retrieved two candles from a cupboard on the other side of the room, the first one pink for true love and the second one red for passion. She placed them in candle holders on her altar and went to the bathroom to prepare for what she hoped was Fate.

❖

Freshly bathed and ready to meet the woman of her dreams, Melody blew out the candles on her altar. She quickly appraised her reflection in the mirror and felt good about herself. She had purposely worn a pentacle necklace, figuring it would be best for everyone to put all her cards on the table. She kissed Pyewackket before locking the door to her apartment behind her and stepped out onto Valencia Street, alive with shoppers and sightseers. Melody loved her neighborhood, which bustled with its shops—a mixture of boutiques, corner groceries, and Latino businesses. Music, reminiscent of other places far removed from San Francisco, floated on the air like a welcome visitor.

At the corner of Valencia and Twenty-first Street she took a right, heading toward the Kitty Kat Lounge. Suddenly, Melody felt that she was being followed. Without trying to appear distressed, she calmly turned her head to determine who was behind her. She was surprised to see a young, blond guy—probably in his twenties. She remembered what Blake had told her about his potential stalker, so she turned around and walked toward the stranger. He stopped as she approached him.

"Hey," she called, refusing to allow herself to feel threatened, "are you the guy who's been stalking my friend?"

Upon being challenged, the blond turned and began to stride in the opposite direction.

"Hey," she called. "Come back here!"

She jogged to catch up, but just as she was about to reach him, he ducked into an alley. Melody hesitated, truly wanting to bust the stalker but not wanting to end up in the hospital. She considered the cell phone in her hand for a moment. She could call the cops, but what would she tell them?

"Shit," she muttered, peering into the alleyway. She couldn't spot the blond, but with all the Dumpsters and discarded boxes, he could have been hiding anywhere. As she turned to go, having recognized the stupidity of risking her life chasing a total stranger who might or might not be stalking Blake, something struck her in the back of the head and she fell.

Melody didn't know how long she had been lying on the sidewalk when she heard a voice somewhere above her.

"Ma'am," the voice said. "Are you all right?"

Melody blinked and the back of her head throbbed as she attempted to sit up.

The voice belonged to a policewoman, and through blurry vision, Melody could see her cruiser pulled over at the curb, lights flashing. Melody rubbed the back of her head and felt a tender bump.

"Somebody hit me in the back of the head," she stammered, fumbling for her cell phone, which had fallen nearby.

"Did you get a good look at them?"

"Yeah, a blond guy, in his twenties, wearing blue jeans and a T-shirt."

"Did he take anything?"

Melody slowly rose and felt in her pocket for her cash. She shook her head. "I still have my cash and cell phone."

"You're a lucky girl. But I'd feel better if you went to the hospital to have that bump looked at."

Melody, her blurry vision fading, saw the officer clearly for the first time. She was probably in her mid to late thirties, pretty and blond. And she was definitely a professional.

"I'm fine," Melody said, smiling. "I just feel a little silly."

"The jerk was probably some homophobe who assumed you were headed to the Kitty Kat Lounge and thought he'd screw with you."

Melody's face warmed. Even though she had been headed to the lounge, she was embarrassed to admit it to the cop.

As she offered her hand to Melody to help her to her feet, Melody smiled again. A pentacle was tattooed on the cop's forearm. "I like your tat," she said, and motioned to her own pentacle necklace.

The cop offered her hand. "My name's Hope."

❖

Blake was in his kitchen tossing a salad when Melody called him with the news. "Are you okay?" he asked. "I can come right over."

"I'm fine, really. But you might want to watch out for this mysterious blond…if it's the same guy."

"It could be a coincidence. I mean, the city's full of blond guys."

"Still, you better watch your back."

"I will, and I'll let my doorman, Mike, know about it."

"Something else happened." Melody was barely able to conceal her excitement.

"What is it? Don't tell me you met someone."

"She's a cop. She came and helped me after the… incident."

"How romantic," Blake kidded her. "Are you going to see her again?"

"She's off work at eleven thirty," Melody said coyly, "and she offered to come by and check on me."

"You'll have to tell me all about it tomorrow." Blake was happy that Melody seemed so excited. The fact that Melody's new interest was a cop reminded him of his failed relationship with Brian, but he didn't voice his doubts.

Melody, however, had already considered the parallel and could sense his hesitation.

"Listen," she said. "I know it might not work out, but she came after I cast a love spell, so I have to give it a shot."

"Of course you do," Blake said. "It's just that I worry about you."

"Don't worry. I'll call you tomorrow."

After hanging up, Blake dialed the front desk and left instructions with Mike that if the blond reappeared, he was to immediately call the police.

❖

The next day was a beautiful, sunny Sunday and Blake awakened earlier than usual, having slept better the previous night than any other in recent memory. He showered, shaved, and quickly dressed, donning jeans, a tight-fitting pullover, and simple black loafers.

In the living room, he carefully placed the first draft of his manuscript into a messenger bag and headed out the door.

Out on the street, the sun just beginning its ascent in the morning sky, Blake was greeted with the sound of a cable car announcing its approach as it climbed nearby California Street. Travelers were just beginning to emerge from the Fairmont Hotel, their cameras strapped around their necks and maps clasped in their hands. Blake could feel their excitement, happy to be in what he considered the most beautiful city in the world, and he enjoyed the enthusiasm they radiated. He turned left on Mason Street, descending the steep hill for his trek to North Beach. On the way he passed the Cable Car Museum, one of the few places in San Francisco he had not investigated but assumed housed spirits. He made a mental note to check out the museum, an easy enough task considering he passed it daily on the way to work.

As he continued, the pungent smell of burning incense filled his nostrils, and he assumed it was coming from the Chinese American family association building across the street. Though he enjoyed Chinatown, with all its shops and restaurants, it was this part of Chinatown—just on the outskirts and mainly residences—that Blake truly loved. This was the true Chinatown, not the carnival-like version peddled to tourists on Grant Avenue. The Chinese Americans lived, played, worked, and died here, and to Blake it was a place of wonder. Little mirrors hung above doorways, meant to deflect evil from the houses they guarded. Foo dogs and lions stood like sentinels at entryways, and oranges sat spiked with countless incense sticks, offerings to the ancestors. Aged grandmothers, stooped and tiny, cautiously made their way down to corner markets in search of fresh produce. As with every other place in the city, spirits wandered the streets here, too.

At Broadway, Blake crossed the street along with the throng of locals and tourists and headed east, in the direction of Columbus Avenue. Here Chinatown merged with the Italian community of North Beach and, in Blake's opinion, was the most vibrant part of the city. Heavy traffic poured out of the Broadway Tunnel, heading toward the bay, and the shops along the wide avenue were alive with the cries of exotic birds and the pungent smells of strange herbs. Warmed by the sun, Blake was almost literally swept along by the human mass surrounding him and, at Columbus Avenue, he turned left. When he entered North Beach proper his senses were stirred by different smells, the smells of coffee and pastries, bars and restaurants. Almost every café in North Beach had tables and chairs placed on the sidewalk in front of it, and, typical of a sunny Sunday in North Beach, nearly every table was packed with customers.

Blake crossed the street at Green and glanced up at his old apartment building, located above the Irish pub. That first year in San Francisco seemed so long ago. How had he ever survived not living in a city? This was his city, and he couldn't conceive of leaving it. On the other side of Green Street, where Green, Columbus, and Stockton streets all intersected, creating a star pattern, Blake spied Donatella, seated at a table in front of Caffe Roma. He crossed Columbus and returned her wave. Given the difficulty in finding unoccupied seats at cafés on weekends, she had probably charmed the table away from some poor, unsuspecting man.

She partially rose and kissed Blake lightly on each cheek. "Welcome back," she said, gesturing to the chair across from her. "Please, sit. I took the liberty of ordering you a latte."

"Thank you." Blake sat, took a sip of the warm, foamy drink, and placed his messenger bag in his lap.

"Here's the manuscript," he said, patting it. "I think you'll be pleased."

"I'm sure I will be. Let's just hope the publisher is, too." She winked at Blake, as if to let him know that she was only joking. "So tell me," she said, changing the subject, "how were your parents?"

"They were fine." Blake gazed across the street at the bakery where he had once worked. "They're older."

Donatella laughed her loud, infectious laugh. "That, my dear boy, is a condition we will all eventually have to face."

"I suppose, but it made me feel guilty for not having visited them sooner."

"Now you will go more often." She took Blake's hand, her expression sympathetic. "And how are you? Are you feeling better about the breakup?"

Blake squeezed Donatella's hand. "I guess, but I'm still

disappointed things didn't work out with Brian. I mean, he was such a nice guy."

"There will be others, believe me," Donatella said.

"I suppose, but what if they have a problem with the ghost thing just like Brian did? Sometimes I wish I'd never been born with this stupid gift."

"Do you remember the night we met?" Donatella had a coy smile on her rouged lips.

"Of course. How could I forget? We were right over there at O'Reilly's."

"That's right. And do you remember what you told me?"

He nodded. "About your grandmother's china?"

"I spent years harboring bad feelings for my sister, not because she took the china, but because I truly believed my grandmother wanted her, and not me, to have it. I assumed that I had somehow angered my grandmother, and it truly hurt me."

"But now you know the truth."

"Now I know the truth, because of you, Blake Danzig."

Blake knew he was blushing, and he nervously toyed with his cup of coffee.

"Don't ever deny your gift. You use it to help people, and they're grateful for that."

"Well," Blake said, uncomfortable with the flattery, "at least Brian and I are still working together. In fact, he's got a new case he wants my help with."

"That's wonderful. I've been married three times, and the only one of my former husbands I would care to see again died."

Blake laughed, and once they had finished their coffee, he walked her to her car, parked around the corner on Union Street.

"I'll look over the manuscript and call you in a couple of days," Donatella said, strapping herself into her seat belt. "Good luck with whatever Brian has for you."

❖

The next morning, as he had promised, Blake phoned Brian at work.

"Hey," Brian said, warmly, "how was New Mexico?"

"I had a good time, but it's good to be back in San Francisco."

"I'll bet. Listen, are you interesting in helping me with another cold case? We're still friends, aren't we?"

"Sure. What is it?"

Instead of explaining over the telephone, Brian suggested that they meet at a location in the Tenderloin, where he would give Blake a rundown on the situation. Blake agreed, and headed down the hill on foot, toward the intersection of Hyde and Eddy streets. Blake loved the Tenderloin, despite its reputation for being a dangerous part of town. With its old architecture, a mixture of Gold Rush style and the later Art Deco, the Tenderloin was what Blake had always imagined a city would be like. And, true to its reputation, the area was home to drug dealers, prostitutes, and countless homeless people. But none of this bothered Blake. As a city dweller, he had quickly learned what everyone referred to as "street smarts," and he knew how to take care of himself. Besides, the Tenderloin was home, too, to a huge immigrant population and it boasted some of the city's best restaurants.

Brian was just parking when Blake arrived, and Blake couldn't help but notice how well he looked. Once again, they exchanged a clumsy hug and Brian led Blake into a nearby apartment building. A sign on the door announced that the building had been condemned. Together they climbed the rickety wooden stairs and finally arrived at the third floor, where Brian led the way down a dark hallway.

"Sorry," he called over his shoulder, "this building is empty and there's no electricity, so watch your step."

The smells in the building, a mixture of urine, backed-up toilets, and rotting food, assailed Blake's senses and he had a coughing fit. A rat scurried by, undeterred.

"You all right?" Brian returned to Blake's side and placed a reassuring hand on his shoulder. "It's pretty rank in here, but we're almost there."

"Sorry. I'm okay."

Brian removed his hand from his shoulder and they continued down the darkened hall. Finally, Brian stopped in front of a door and shined a small penlight on it, which illuminated a tarnished number, 308.

He pushed the door open and light from a window inside flooded into the hallway. Blake followed Brian into the barren unit, happy to be able to see clearly again.

Plaster hung precariously from the ceiling. Faded, water-stained wallpaper hung in strips from the walls, and a broken window allowed in cool, fresh air. From the droppings on the ruined floor, it was evident pigeons roosted there at night.

"The building is supposed to be condemned," Brian explained, "but the homeless and the drug dealers sneak in through the basement and sleep here."

The thought of being the only two people in the building besides a bunch of drug dealers frightened Blake more than any ghost could, even if Brian was carrying a gun. "What's the deal with this place?" He started at a sound from the hallway.

"Relax. It's probably just the rats."

"That's comforting."

"Back in eighty-four, there were a series of murders in this area," Brian said. "One of the victims was killed here in what was once her apartment."

"And the case was never solved?"

"No, not officially. The story was fed to the newspapers that the killings were part of a drug war in the Tenderloin, a war that the SFPD finally got a handle on. But the killer was never officially found and the case was closed."

"Why reopen it now? If people believed it was all part of a drug war, why pursue it?"

"Chief Norris was impressed that we cracked the Doodler case, and he wants us to do the same with a handful of other ones."

Blake nodded and walked into a neighboring room, his footsteps echoing on the hardwood floors. The room, its condition as dismal as the first, was long and narrow.

"That was the bedroom," Brian called, "where the victim was murdered."

Blake turned to face Brian and, as he did, noticed movement in his peripheral vision. As he peered back into the room, he saw that a closet door had partially closed. Cautiously, he approached the door, his breath visible in the air.

"It just got really cold in here," he told Brian, who remained standing just outside the door to the bedroom. It reminded Blake why their relationship hadn't worked out.

Blake grasped the cold doorknob and slowly pulled the door open. There, standing in the shadows, was the ghost of a young woman, her hair short and dyed bright red. She was dressed in a black T-shirt, a black leather miniskirt, red fishnet stockings, and patent-leather ankle boots. Her black T-shirt had long, horizontal slashes across the front, and Blake wasn't sure if this was part of eighties fashion or of the crime itself.

At first, the spirit looked terrified, but apparently when she realized Blake meant her no harm, she began to speak. Unfortunately, there was a problem.

"Um, Brian," Blake said, turning away from the spirit, "there's a ghost here, all right, but she's not speaking English."

"Shit. The victim was Ukrainian, an immigrant. It never occurred to me—"

"Can we get a translator? I can try to repeat what I'm hearing."

"I'll put in a request tomorrow." The frustration was showing on Brian's face.

Without saying another word, they began the long, dark walk back through the deserted building, leaving the pitiful spirit alone.

Once they were back outside in front of the building, Blake grabbed Brian's hand.

"Listen, it'll be fine. I mean, there is a ghost there and, if she's willing to talk, you'll get your killer."

Brian nodded and said, "I've missed your optimism."

"How would you like to have dinner tonight, Brian?"

Brian's hand went limp in Blake's, and he averted his gaze to the sidewalk. "Listen, Blake," his voice was low, "I've been meaning to tell you something."

Blake stared at him, unsure of what was coming next.

Brian cleared his throat and looked him right in the eye. "I'm seeing someone," he said, almost apologetically. "I met him a little over a week ago. I meant to tell you, but just didn't know how."

Blake released Brian's hand and hoped his voice wouldn't betray his disappointment. Even though he had done his share of sleeping around since their breakup, Blake still hoped he and Brian might somehow reconcile. Now, with three little words, it seemed as if it was gone.

"Oh, that's great," he lied, trying to act as if he had just heard good news.

"I'm really sorry—"

"Brian, don't apologize. I'm happy for you."

"If you don't want to work on this case, I totally understand."

"Don't be stupid," Blake said, a little too harshly. "We're broken up, right? That's all there is to it. You've moved on and I need to get used to it."

When Brian didn't reply, Blake nodded, realizing what he said was true. It was time to move on. "Call me when you find an interpreter. I'll be here."

He began his long trek back up the hill, leaving Brian standing beside his car.

Chapter Twelve

As soon as Blake returned to the safety of his apartment, he called Melody. He didn't really want to bother her during her week off, but after Brian's confession, he didn't know where else to turn. Fortunately, she answered quickly and sounded almost giddy.

"What's up?" she asked.

"You sure sound happy." He hated himself for his self-pity.

"I am. And, as of last night, I'm officially dating again."

"That's great," Blake said, trying to sound supportive. "So you and your cop hit it off?"

"Her name is Hope and she's great. She's really beautiful, has a great sense of humor, and," Melody paused for dramatic effect, "the witchcraft thing doesn't freak her out at all."

"I just saw Brian."

"How'd that go?" Melody's tone was cautious.

"He's started seeing someone."

"Oh, Blake. I'm so sorry. Are you okay?"

"It was just a surprise." Blake sighed. "But, yeah, I'm fine."

"Do you want me to come over? I really don't mind."

"No. I'm fine, even though he had the nerve to ask if I still wanted to work with him on cases."

"Do you?"

"Of course." Blake was miffed she would even question him. "The cases we help the department solve don't just benefit the police. They help families get closure."

"I still think Brian's question was a valid one. But I do know you take your job seriously, so he shouldn't have assumed otherwise."

"Well," Blake said, tired of the topic, "when do you see Hope again?"

"Tonight. I'm making dinner here."

"Nice. Have a good evening and let me know how it goes."

"I will. Do you mind if I bring Hope over for ghost-show night?"

"No. I'm dying to meet her."

Ghost-show night, as they referred to Tuesday nights, was when a series of paranormal investigation shows aired on one of the cable networks, and they got together to watch, if only to compare notes. Usually, they watched just to laugh at Clive Damon's *Haunted Isle*.

As he hung up, Blake couldn't help but feel a bit jealous of Melody's new love affair. Then again, he reminded himself, Melody had been single for such a long time that she—of all people—deserved a hot love affair.

Fuck Brian and his new boyfriend. The new guy's probably got the personality of a beer can.

And anyway, why was he still jealous? Brian had made it perfectly clear it was over, and it had been long enough for Blake to get used to the idea. Besides, Blake had certainly used the time since the split to his advantage, so why couldn't he let Brian see other men? But Blake wasn't out searching for a relationship, just a little physical interaction. What Brian had done was different, and it felt strangely like a betrayal.

Blake grabbed a light jacket and went downstairs in search of a taxi.

❖

After mulling over the millions of possibilities, Blake ended up at the Bayside Bar, his usual haunt. The bartender that Monday night was a new one—at least one Blake had never seen before—and as the bar was fairly slow, he chatted amiably with Blake. He introduced himself as Joe, was in his late twenties or early thirties—Blake couldn't tell—and had medium brown hair and blue eyes. He was good-looking and, although he stood only about five feet nine inches tall, the way his T-shirt and jeans hugged his body suggested that he worked out religiously.

Blake glanced around the nearly empty bar, assessing the situation. The only other patrons were either together, not Blake's type, or too drunk to be of any use for what Blake had in mind. That left Joe.

"So," he said, flashing his most charming smile at the bartender, "you married?"

"Just got out of a relationship," he replied, good-naturedly, as he washed dirty pint glasses. "That's why I took this job."

"To meet men?" Blake sipped his beer.

"To pay bills." Joe laughed. "I have another job waiting tables, but the rent on my apartment is just too much for one person."

Blake admired his honesty.

"How about you?" Joe asked. "Are you married?"

"Just got out of a relationship." Blake parroted Joe's reply to the same question.

"Can I ask you something?" Joe leaned in close.

Blake nodded, curious as to what the question might be.

"Who broke up? Was it you or your boyfriend?"

"He did." Blake didn't know why this admission made him feel so guilty. Why was it so much more shameful to be the one who was dumped, as opposed to being the one who did the dumping? Was it because it implied that, if you get dumped, you are somehow flawed, incapable of being loved?

"Me, too," Joe confessed. "He said he didn't feel like we wanted the same things."

Blake had to laugh. After all, when you got right down to it, wasn't that the reason any relationship didn't work out, no matter what you called it?

"Yeah," Joe said. "I mean I wanted a partner who loved me and who I could love back. I wanted to grow old together and send out stupid Christmas cards together, and to go on vacations together. Hell, I even wanted all of the shit that comes with it, like in-laws and silly arguments."

"Is he seeing someone else?" Blake asked.

Joe seemed stunned by the question and straightened his back. "I…I don't know," he said, sadness clouding his handsome face.

"Mine is," Blake said, almost sorry he had caused distress. "I just found out today."

"That really sucks." Joe placed a fresh beer in front of Blake. "This is on me."

Suddenly, the jukebox in the corner came to life, blaring

Depeche Mode. Joe reached for a button behind the counter and turned the volume down.

"I swear," he said, shaking his head, "that damned ghost is driving me crazy."

It took Blake a moment to comprehend what Joe had said. He stared at the handsome bartender and slowly grinned. "Did you say 'ghost'?"

Joe laughed and busied himself by wiping down a section of bar that looked otherwise spotless. "I know," he said, "people think I'm crazy, but strange things happen in here, especially around closing time."

"Like what?"

Joe ran down the laundry list of paranormal manifestations: glasses moving on their own volition, lights that stayed neither on nor off, doors that opened and closed when no one was there, and the jukebox with a mind of its own.

"Have you ever seen an apparition?" Blake asked.

"No." Joe seemed happy someone was taking him seriously. "I don't know if I want to."

"It's not as bad as you might think."

Joe stared at Blake for a moment, as if unsure if he was being serious. "You see ghosts?" he finally managed.

"I own a business that does paranormal investigations," he said, matter-of-factly. "I deal with ghosts all the time."

"Wait a minute," a flicker of recognition showed on his face, "what did you say your name was?"

"Blake. Blake Danzig."

"Holy shit, I thought I recognized you! I've seen your show a few times, but never thought I'd actually be serving you beers."

Blake was flattered. While he normally tried to avoid

drawing attention to himself in public, tonight his ego needed stroking and he gladly accepted it.

"So, Joe, you believe in ghosts?"

Joe nodded, his expression serious.

"When I was a kid," he explained, again leaning in close, "we lived in this old farmhouse that was totally haunted. I've been a believer for as long as I can remember."

"Lots of people don't believe. In fact, that's why my last boyfriend left me. He *did* believe and said the whole ghost thing freaked him out."

"His loss." Joe looked at Blake in a way that suggested he was willing to serve Blake more than beers.

"What time do you get off work?"

A few hours later, during the cab ride up to Blake's Nob Hill condominium, he and Joe found it difficult to keep their hands off one another. But the cab driver, a salty, older man in his sixties, kept glaring at them in the rearview mirror, so they did their best to behave. Once inside Blake's apartment, however, they acted like two starving men and hungrily tugged at belt buckles, buttons, and shoelaces, groping and kissing one another until both were naked and writhing on the sofa. Blake was pleased to discover Joe was endowed with a very large cock, and he had been right about the firm body, barely concealed under the tight-fitting clothes. He greedily took Joe's fat cock into his mouth and down his throat. Joe reciprocated by sucking Blake's large boner and they lay on the sofa sixty-nining each other until Joe suddenly stopped and whispered to Blake, "You want to fuck?"

Blake stopped and looked up at Joe. Suddenly, the angst he had felt over Brian earlier in the day was gone. Here he was with this hot, young guy who was totally into him and not afraid of ghosts. What had he been thinking?

"Sure," he said, inhaling the manly, musky scent of Joe's balls, "there are condoms in the bedroom."

He got up from the sofa and led Joe into the other room. Joe crawled onto the bed and watched as Blake bent over his nightstand.

"You like to top or bottom?" he asked, his hands clasped behind his head.

"I'm usually top," Blake said, holding a condom, "but I'm versatile, so whatever you want is fine with me."

He glanced at Joe's meaty boner. *Bottom would be just fine.*

"Fuck me," Joe said.

Blake didn't argue and unrolled the latex sheath over his hard-on. He squeezed a bit of lubricant onto his rubbered dick and spread some more onto Joe's asshole. Then he climbed onto the bed and lifted Joe's legs over his muscular forearms and gently pressed his cock against Joe's hole.

"Yeah," Joe said, his nipples erect, "stick it in…fuck me."

Blake thrust his hips forward and felt Joe's tight hole enveloping his stiff shaft. "Shit, that feels good," he said.

"Yeah? You like that tight ass?"

"Yeah." Blake leaned closer and kissed Joe on the mouth. He was keeping his strokes long and slow, relishing the tightness enveloping his cock. "You like that cock in your ass, baby?" he teased.

"It's filling me up." Joe lifted his legs higher on Blake's arms, opening up wider for the stiff dick inside him.

"Shit," Blake said, "that feels nice."

Suddenly, unable to hold back any longer, Joe shot a hot load, which streamed across his chest and splattered his face.

"Fuck, yeah," Blake said. "Here I come, baby."

Later, as Joe lay sleeping in the crook of his arm snoring softly, Blake felt content. His day had certainly improved, there was no doubt. He craned his neck and kissed the top of Joe's head. Could he be the one, the guy that was willing to stay with him, ghosts or no ghosts? He wasn't sure and was unwilling to rush into anything. That much he had learned from his failed relationship with Brian. Still, the possibility was there, and it filled him with a renewed faith in love, in fate, maybe. He drifted off to sleep, happy and content just to be in the moment.

When he awoke the next morning the sun was shining through the bedroom window and Blake felt more rested than he had in a very long time. Joe was just emerging from the bathroom, still naked, and Blake gazed at the beautiful body approaching his bed.

"Sorry to wake you up," Joe said. He slipped gingerly back into bed next to Blake and kissed him on the lips. "I've got to get to work."

"You weren't going to leave without saying good-bye, were you?" Blake asked.

"No. You looked so cute sleeping, I hated to disturb you."

They kissed again, this time longer. When they finished, their eyes met.

"Look," Blake said, searching for the right words. "I know that we've both just recently gotten out of relationships, but..." He faltered. Was he ready to try again? And, for that matter, was Joe?

"Can we do this again?" Joe asked. "I really like you, Blake."

Blake laughed, grateful that Joe had said what he wanted

to hear, grateful that he had been spared the burden of asking for another try.

"I was hoping you'd say that. I really like you, too."

"I've written my cell phone number down. It's on your dresser. Please call me."

They kissed one more time, then Joe rose from the bed and dressed quickly, already late for his job waiting tables. Blake closed the door behind him after he left and went to the kitchen for a cup of coffee. He had just taken his first sip when the phone rang. It was Brian, and he answered.

"Blake. I got a translator and wondered if you'd meet me back at the apartment building."

"Of course." The previous night's fuck had eradicated Blake's resentment. "Just say when."

They agreed to meet in one hour, and Blake showered and dressed. He picked up the piece of paper with Joe's number from the top of his dresser and tucked it into his wallet. As silly as it might have seemed, just having the number so close made him feel somehow invincible, almost as if as long as he had the number, he had Joe. And that made him feel like anything was possible, that nothing—no matter how dire it might seem—could ruin his day. After a quick ride in the elevator, he was greeted by Mike, the doorman.

"Good morning, Mr. Danzig," he said, cheerfully. "So I guess we were wrong about the blond guy who came to see you when you were gone."

"I'm sorry?" Blake replied.

"The guy we thought was a stalker," Mike explained. "I saw him getting out of the taxi with you and that other guy last night. I guess he was a friend, after all. Sorry about that."

Blake's mind was racing. Could the mysterious blond have been the ghost from the Bayside Bar? And if it was, why could Mike see and even talk to him? The fact Blake hadn't seen or even sensed him in the taxi the previous night was equally puzzling. A mysterious blond had attacked Melody. Blake thanked Mike and stepped out onto the sidewalk. He pulled Joe's number from his wallet and entered the number into his cell phone. Unfortunately, he was sent straight to voice mail.

"Listen, Joe," he said, trying to measure his words carefully. "It's Blake. I know this is going to sound weird, and I'll explain later, but be very careful around the ghost at the Bayside." He hesitated a moment, unsure of what else to say. "Let me know when you get this message."

He ended the call and looked around for any signs of the mysterious blond, but nothing seemed out of the ordinary. Was it possible he had a spirit stalker? Anything was possible in the paranormal world, and it certainly wasn't unusual for a ghost to manifest to whomever it chose. Still, a ghost stalker certainly seemed a stretch. Blake did his best to push it out of his mind and began his walk down the hill to meet Brian. When he arrived at the abandoned apartment building, Brian was waiting for him by his car.

"Thanks for coming on such short notice," he said.

"No problem. Where's the interpreter?"

"She should be here any minute. Listen, Blake, I wanted to apologize about yesterday. I guess I didn't realize how you'd take the news of me dating someone else."

Blake touched Brian's arm, stopping him. He was feeling too good, despite the recent news of a phantom stalker, to let Brian feel guilty.

"You don't have to apologize. It's not like I didn't know that we were broken up. I guess the hard thing for me—

especially given the reason why we didn't work out—is that I assume the guy after me will be better than me."

Blake considered telling Brian he, too, had met someone, but decided against it, not wanting to turn the whole thing into some stupid contest. Brian didn't answer and seemed relieved when the interpreter joined them.

"Detective Cox?" she asked, looking from Brian to Blake.

"I'm Detective Cox." Brian offered his hand. "And this is Blake Danzig."

"Linda Harris." The interpreter, a small, mousy-looking woman in her twenties, shook Blake's hand. She looked like she would frighten easily, and Blake wondered how she would handle being confronted by a ghost.

As if reading his mind, Brian leaned close to Blake. "Don't worry," he said. "I briefed Linda on the whole thing by phone. She knows."

"I'm a big girl," she said. "And, by the way, I'm a big fan of your show."

"Thanks."

They entered the building and followed the same route Blake and Brian had taken two days earlier, carefully walking through the darkened hallways and finally arriving at unit 308. Blake strode confidently into the bedroom and opened the closet door. For a moment he thought the ghost was gone, but as his eyes began to adjust the shadows, he could see her, hiding in a corner.

"Who are you?" he asked. Linda, standing just behind him, translated the question into Ukrainian.

The ghost's expression changed upon hearing her native language, and she stepped cautiously from the shadows.

"We're here to help you," Blake said. "Please, tell us your name."

Again, Linda translated.

"Anya," the spirit replied. Blake repeated this to his companions and Brian nodded—they had the right spirit.

"Who did this to you?" Blake asked.

Once Linda had translated the question, the spirit began to speak quickly, her eyes huge.

"Slowly," he said, kindly.

But the ghost seemed eager to tell her story to the first people willing to listen in over twenty years.

"I don't know," Blake said. "I wish you could hear her, Linda. I'm having difficulty making out what she's saying."

Brian sighed impatiently behind them.

"What does it sound like she's saying?" Linda acted as if she was beginning to feel a little spooked.

Blake wasn't thrilled about the prospect of performing a phonetic translation. Too many things could go wrong and, since he didn't speak a word of Ukrainian, the ghost might as well have been speaking Swahili. To make matters worse, she had begun to sob uncontrollably, choking out each foreign word between sobs.

"I don't know," Blake said, feeling horribly self-conscious. "It sounds like '*vil a mean-ya vladealitz.*'"

The ghost nodded at Blake, and Linda asked Blake to repeat what he had just said, his tongue twisting on the strange words. Suddenly, Linda repeated perfectly what the ghost had been saying. The ghost nodded. *"Da, da!"*

Linda turned to Brian. "That means 'my landlord killed me,'" she said, her expression grave. She turned back to Blake. "Are you sure?"

"The ghost says yes," Blake replied. He was suddenly

struck with an idea and turned to Brian. "Do you have a pen?"

Brian fished around in his pocket and finally produced a ballpoint, which he passed to Blake. Blake, in turn, offered the pen to the ghost.

"Can you write that?" he asked.

Linda translated and gasped when the pen floated through what looked like thin air.

"Okay," she said, now acting very frightened, "that's creepy."

"Write what you told us," Blake said, "on the wall."

Linda translated his instructions and the pen—seemingly of its own volition—began to form Cyrillic characters on the closet wall in front of them.

Linda read aloud after the pen tumbled to the floor. "'My landlord killed me. He was a monster and killed many women here.'"

"Holy shit," Brian whispered. He turned and walked into the empty living room.

Blake and Linda joined him.

"How do we prove that?" Brian asked. He gestured wildly in the direction of the bedroom.

"She told us," Blake said. "Isn't that enough?"

"No," Brian replied flatly. "I can't obtain an arrest warrant on the word of a spirit. They'd lock me up in the nearest loony bin and throw away the key."

Welcome to my world, Blake thought. "I have an idea," he said. "What if the cops overlooked the writing on the wall back in 1984? You came here to look into the old case, found the writing, and hired Linda to translate it."

Brian looked skeptical. "It's a long shot," he said, "but it's worth a try."

"I'll vouch for you," Linda said. Then, looking around the room, she added, "Can we go now? This turned out to be a little more than I bargained for."

"Not yet," Blake said. "We need to do something first."

Brian and Linda stared at him, clearly confused. He walked back into the bedroom and stopped in front of the open closet door. The ghost, who seemed to have regained her composure, looked at him.

"Tell her she's free to move on now," Blake told Linda. "Thanks to her we will catch and punish the man who did this to her."

Linda translated and Anya looked at Blake, confusion on her face.

"Anya," Blake said. "You're free. Go now and rest in peace."

She seemed to have understood Blake, because she beamed, then began to fade from sight even before Linda began translating.

"She's gone," Blake announced. He retrieved Brian's pen from the floor and handed it to him.

Brian seemed reluctant to touch the object, as if the ghost had somehow contaminated it, but quickly shoved it into his pocket.

He promised to call Blake as soon as they knew anything more, and they parted in front of the building. As Blake made his way back up the hill, his cell phone began to ring. To his great relief, Blake saw it was Joe.

"Sorry to just now get back to you," said Joe. "I'm one of those rare people that actually turns his phone off at work."

"That's okay. I'm just glad to hear your voice."

"What were you saying about the ghost at the bar?" Joe sounded amused.

"This is going to sound weird," Blake said, "but I think the ghost at the Bayside might be stalking me."

"What? Are you kidding?"

"No. "Listen, when can I see you again, Joe? I'd really rather talk about this in person."

"How about tonight?"

"Be at my place by eight. My friend Melody and her new girlfriend will be there, too. You can meet everybody and I'll explain about the ghost."

Chapter Thirteen

Blake busily tidied up his condominium in preparation for the arrival of his guests. Ghost-show night had never been a formal affair, just he and Melody sharing wine and appetizers while critiquing competing paranormal shows. This night, however, had to be special. Not only would he meet Melody's new love interest, Hope, but Melody would meet Joe. Part of Blake felt that it might be premature to introduce Joe to his best friend—they had only spent one night together, after all—but his real inspiration for having Joe over had more to do with the ghost at the bar. Besides, he told himself, maybe Joe *could* be the right guy. Might as well get introductions out of the way and see where things go from there.

Blake walked to the kitchen and opened the refrigerator, checking there was enough wine being chilled, and pulled out a platter of cheeses he had assembled earlier. From a nearby paper bag he produced a baguette, which he cut into bite-sized pieces and placed on a separate platter alongside a variety of gourmet crackers. He checked the clock on the wall and, seeing he still had plenty of time to shower before the guests arrived, retrieved a vase from a cupboard for the bouquet of irises he had purchased at the corner market just down the hill. He carried his arrangement into the living room, placed it on the coffee table, and admired his handiwork. Satisfied the place was ready for company, he went to shower.

❖

The subway car was filled to capacity, forcing Joe to stand for the short ride downtown. Grasping the overhead railing in one hand for support and, in the other, clutching the bouquet of roses he had purchased from a vendor outside the Castro station, Joe took in his fellow passengers: a mixture of business men and women in their corporate drag, shoppers laden with bags of loot, kids from the suburbs in town to cause a little trouble, and students heading home from school. They were like ants going about their business in seemingly disorganized chaos.

Joe stepped off of the cramped subway car at the Powell Street station, below Market Street. The ride from Castro Street had been a quick one. At first he'd been hesitant about bringing flowers, but had given in to his urge in the end. Besides, they were yellow roses, and if he remembered his flower etiquette properly, yellow roses symbolized friendship. Anyway, he wanted to make a good impression, and wasn't it customary to bring gifts when invited to another person's house?

At the top of the escalator leading from the subway stop to the street, Joe emerged at the Powell Street cable-car turnaround. Surrounded by tourists from every corner of the earth waiting for their turn on the famous cable cars, he grinned at their enthusiasm and took in the sounds and smells of the city. He continued past Union Square and the Academy of Art building, turned left at California Street, and began climbing another steep street, slowly making his way to Blake's building.

❖

Melody and Hope sat in the backseat of a taxi, headed downtown. Melody glanced over at Hope, who looked ill at ease, and squeezed her hand. "Are you nervous about meeting Blake?"

"A little. I mean, not only is he your best friend, he's also Blake Danzig, star of his own television show."

"Hey, I'm on that show, too."

"I know." Hope kissed her on the lips and glanced at the cab driver. He was focused on the road, busy concentrating on the traffic. She squeezed Melody's hand and looked out the window.

Melody settled back into the seat, still grasping Hope's hand. Hope seemed so far away, staring silently out the window. What could be bothering her? Surely she wasn't all that nervous about meeting Blake, who was one of the kindest, most down-to-earth people possible. But if Blake wasn't the issue, what was? It certainly didn't seem to be the witchcraft thing. Hope seemed downright supportive of whatever Melody wanted to believe. She had even agreed to wear the protective amulet that Melody had given her "just in case." The night they met, Melody had inquired about the pentacle tattooed on Hope's arm and she had shrugged, explaining that it had more to do with her heavy metal days than with witchcraft. Still, she had been willing to entertain the notion of goddess worship.

And that was enough for now.

As was her way, Melody began worrying about the fledgling relationship. Had she done something wrong? Had the talisman been too much too soon? And, if it was, what could she do to fix things? One thing she knew for certain:

she would not let this relationship go without a fight, and she would even use magic if necessary.

❖

Blake answered the knock on his door, and Joe held out the bouquet of yellow roses and kissed Blake softly on the lips.

"I'm glad you got here first," Blake said, leading Joe to the kitchen before he searched for another vase. "At least I'll get you to myself for a little while."

He put the roses in another vase, which he placed in the middle of the dining-room table, then rejoined Joe, who had remained in the kitchen. "Thank you for the flowers," he said, putting his arms around Joe, "they're beautiful."

"What was that crazy call about?" Joe arched an eyebrow. "Something about the ghost at the bar?"

"I'll tell you when Melody gets here." He poured two glasses of wine, offered one to Joe, and they both took a sip.

"Whatever it is," Joe said, "I'm glad to see you again."

"Me, too."

Unfortunately, a second knock on the door interrupted their brief private time, and, without waiting for a reply, Melody and Hope entered the apartment. "Hello?" Melody called. "We're here."

"In the kitchen." Blake stole one more kiss from Joe before stepping around the corner. Joe followed him, wineglass in hand.

Introductions were made, and Blake instantly liked Hope. She seemed intelligent and possessed a pronounced sense of self-confidence that came across as neither smug nor pushy. Upon meeting Joe, Melody raised her eyebrows at Blake, an amused look on her face. They left Joe and Hope to chat and went to the kitchen to pour two more glasses of wine.

"When did you meet Joe?" she asked, keeping her voice low.

"Last night." Blake ignored Melody's wicked smile. "He's cute, don't you think?"

"Very." Melody peered into the living room, where Hope and Joe were admiring the view from the windows. "What do you think of Hope?"

"She seems very nice." Blake said, passing a wineglass to Melody.

"And gorgeous." She sounded slighted.

"And gorgeous." Blake laughed. "If you like girls."

He carried the second glass of wine into the living room and offered it to Hope. "Okay," he said, looking from Melody to Joe. "Something weird happened last night you should both know about."

He explained what Mike, the doorman, had told him about the previous night's arriving cab—namely, that three people emerged from the cab instead of two. "I believe it was the ghost from the Bayside Bar."

"Okay, that's a little weird, isn't it?" Melody slowly took a seat on the sofa, where Hope joined her, but remained silent.

"Well, yes," Blake said. "But it's not unheard of for ghosts to attach themselves to people they are somehow attracted to. Or even—as in the case of my doorman—to appear to whomever they choose."

"But you didn't see him?" Melody asked.

Blake shook his head, feeling serious.

"A ghost stalker." Melody laughed. "Leave it to you."

"It's not really that funny. I think the ghost is the blond who attacked you Sunday night."

"Blake, this guy was real—"

"He had an average build, was in his twenties, and he was wearing faded jeans and a white T-shirt?"

"This is too weird." Melody said, and Hope put an arm around her.

Joe took his cue to chime in. "That's why you told me to be careful at the bar. You think he'd attack me?"

"Yes. The first night I saw him, he definitely seemed interested in me. In fact, I think he was trying to get me to follow him to the bathroom."

"A gay ghost," Melody said, almost to herself. "That's fucking creepy."

"Why not? And I'm afraid that if he finds out you're dating me," Blake addressed Joe, "he might try to harm you like he did Melody."

"I already told you," Joe said, "I'm not afraid of ghosts."

"Still, I think I should go to the bar and try to get rid of him."

"How are you going to manage that, Blake?" Joe asked.

"I don't know, but, if it's all right with you, I'd like to meet you at the bar after you close tomorrow night and maybe have a talk with our otherworldly stalker."

"Okay." Then, with a wide grin, Joe said, "Cool, I get to see you in action, and not on television."

❖

With plans made, the four of them settled in front of the television for a night of paranormal television.

"Is your show on tonight?" asked Joe, who had curled up next to Blake.

"No. We're on another network."

"Most of the other paranormal investigative shows, which air on a rival network," Melody explained, "are a mixture of different guys doing basically the same thing—some better than others."

"The first show," Blake said, "is *Ghost Nation*, which is made up of three guys who used simple, handheld cameras to record their investigations. The leader of the group is well-built and not unattractive, but he looks like a wannabe porn star. And the way he butchers the English language is so past laughable, it's sad."

"I swear, you guys," Melody said, mimicking their rival, "I seen a ghost in there!"

Blake agreed. "It amazes me that such a big, dumb frat boy could have ended up with his own show. They do manage to catch some fascinating footage of spirits on camera, so I'm willing to overlook his battering of the English language."

Two regular guys headed the next show. When not working their day jobs as bus drivers, they starred on the show named after the paranormal investigations company they'd formed called T.A.G.S., an acronym for The American Ghost Society. Blake particularly liked this show and its stars and was constantly impressed with their innovative approaches to gathering paranormal evidence. In one episode, they sprinkled baby powder in a hallway frequented by a poltergeist and, amazingly, captured footprints in the otherwise-deserted hall.

In the third show, a group of hysterical college-aged kids failed—that night anyway—to capture anything of value. To Blake, they seemed to be playing with fire, and he questioned the wisdom of the show's producers to put such innocents in harm's way. With any luck, the show wouldn't make it to a second season.

The final show of the evening was *Haunted Isle*, Clive

Damon's vehicle for paranormal investigation. As usual, the location of that night's show was an ancient castle, this one somewhere in Scotland. In the end, the camera recorded no concrete evidence of ghostly presence.

As the show was ending, footage—seemingly live, as opposed to the taped show that had just aired—appeared on-screen. Clive Damon, dressed in some sort of ridiculous Western getup, smiled at his television audience. "Thank you for watching tonight's show," he drawled. "I certainly hope you enjoyed the investigation and invite you to tune in for our next show, filmed in the American Southwest, site of numerous hauntings."

Melody scoffed. "What's that fraud doing in America? Not enough ghosts in merry old England?"

Blake shushed her as Clive continued speaking. "And I would like to thank my esteemed colleague, Blake Danzig," his smile looked almost painful, "who was kind enough to show me a wonderful time during my visit to New Mexico."

Melody gave Blake a curious look, and he avoided her eyes.

"What the hell did that mean?" she asked.

"We had a couple of drinks. That's all." Blake felt sheepish.

As the show's theme music cued up and credits began flashing on the screen, Blake rose and walked to the kitchen, empty wineglass in hand.

Melody followed him. "A couple of drinks? You can't stand that man."

Hope and Joe watched the exchange from their seats, clearly amused.

"Melody," Blake sighed, "he was there and I was there. It was a weird coincidence, but I had to be polite."

Melody's expression softened from disgust to something that looked like pity. "You're too nice," she said, emptying the remains of a wine bottle into her glass.

"He suggested that we team up." Blake walked back to the sofa and sat next to Joe. "But I think the wine was talking. He didn't say anything specific."

Melody sat back down next to Hope and shook her head. "Our show's so much better than his, I can't imagine him having the nerve to think you'd be interested. In my opinion, the two bus drivers from *T.A.G.S.* are way better than his show."

"I agree," Blake said.

"Do you realize," Joe looked at his watch, "that we just sat through four hours of television?"

Blake and Melody shared a guilty look. "It's serious research for us," Blake said. "We do it every Tuesday."

Hope looked at her own watch. "I should really be getting home. I have an early day tomorrow."

"I'll get us a cab," Melody said, rising from the sofa.

"What about you?" Blake asked Joe. "Do you need to get home, or do you want to stay?"

Joe kissed Blake on the neck and whispered, "I'll stay if you like. I wouldn't mind repeating last night."

Blake walked Melody and Hope to the door. "Call me tomorrow," he said as he kissed Melody's cheek. "It was wonderful to meet you, Hope."

The two women boarded the elevator.

Blake locked the door behind them and went back to the living room, where Joe was gathering wineglasses and plates. "I had a really good time tonight," Joe said.

"Me, too." Blake wrapped his arms around Joe's muscular torso. "Put those dishes down. The night's fun is just getting started."

CHAPTER FOURTEEN

Blake woke before Joe the next morning. Joe groaned lightly as Blake freed his arm from under him and got up. As Blake stood at the sink brushing his teeth, he felt content. Not only had everyone seemed to have gotten along the night before, but the sex with Joe had been amazing. But was he moving too quickly? When Blake walked back into the bedroom, Joe was still sleeping. He entertained crawling back into the bed and waking him, but decided against it. Instead, he pulled on a pair of boxer briefs and began gathering up the neglected dishes from the previous night's gathering. He had just finished loading the dishwasher when Joe entered, looking adorable with his messy hair. Unfortunately, Joe had put on his underwear and T-shirt.

"Good morning." Blake kissed Joe on the lips. "Would you like a cup of coffee?"

"Good morning." Joe yawned. "No. I haven't slept at home for two days and I should probably go."

Blake nodded. He would be gracious and not show his disappointment. "I don't blame you." He kissed Joe again and poured himself a cup. "I had another good time last night."

"I did, too. Your friend Melody and her girlfriend were really cool people."

"Yeah," Blake said. "I meant I had a good time after Melody and Hope left."

"Oh…that…" Joe winked at him. "It was good, too."

Blake gazed at Joe for a moment, slowly licking his lips. He put his cup on the counter, but before he could move, Joe was already running toward the bedroom. When Blake caught up with him they both collapsed, laughing, on the bed.

And it only took a minute to strip off their underwear.

"Promise you'll call as soon as your shift is over," Blake said, once they were dressing once again.

"I will."

"And promise me you'll be very careful around that psychotic spirit."

"I ain't afraid of no ghost," Joe said jokingly.

"Promise."

"I promise. I'll be very careful."

After Joe had gone, Blake was pulling on a pair of jeans when the telephone in the living room rang. He answered on the third ring.

"It's Brian." Blake could hear excitement in Brian's voice.

"What's up?" he asked, buttoning his jeans.

"You'll never believe it, but we arrested the former landlord from that abandoned building and the guy actually confessed to the murders."

"Seriously?" Their gamble had paid off.

"The guy seemed proud he had killed so many prostitutes," Brian said. "He acted like we should have been awarding him a medal or something."

"And the writing on the closet wall?"

"I played it off like you said. Everybody assumes it was a

clue the police missed back at the time of the murders. I told the chief you were psychically drawn to the closet, which was how we found it."

"Thanks, and congratulations on catching the bad guy."

"I couldn't have done it without you, Blake."

They were silent for a moment. "Well, I should go," Brian said. "I'll call you if any new cold-case files come across my desk."

"I'll do whatever I can. Bye."

Blake hung up and returned to the bedroom, where he pulled a light blue button-down from the closet. As he fastened the shirt, he felt relieved that, thanks to Joe, Brian no longer had a hold over him.

He slipped on a pair of sneakers and walked out the front door, which he locked behind him. It had been over a week since he had been to his office, and he was determined to put in a real day's work. At the very least, he would pay attention to the bills.

He tossed a stack of unopened mail on the floor onto his already cluttered desk. The light on the answering machine was blinking, Blake pushed the "play" button and sat down as the playbacks began. The first message was a sales call, and Blake hit the "skip" button. The next one was from one of the local television stations interested in an interview, and he grabbed a pen and copied down the caller's name and number, which he would pass along to Donatella.

The third and last message was from an obviously distressed woman. "My name is Ellen," she said. "I need for you to come to my house…" Blake thought for a moment she had hung up.

"Look," she finally said. "I don't really believe in this

ghost nonsense, but something's in my house." The woman left a telephone number and hung up.

Blake dialed it and said to the woman who answered on the second ring, "I'm returning a call from Ellen. This is Danzig Paranormal Investigations."

"This is Ellen. Something's very wrong with my multimillion-dollar town house on Lombard Street. And while I hesitate to attribute anything to ghosts, I'm absolutely terrified by recent events."

"What sort of things are you experiencing? I mean, if you're not sure the activity is paranormal, why call us?"

His question was borderline rude, but nonbelievers always pissed him off. Ellen seemed to bristle at his question. Blake wasn't sure whether the woman was angry or distraught, but her reply was terse.

"When can you come over? You'll see what I mean."

"I can come over right now, if that works for you."

The woman agreed and Blake jotted down the address, grateful for an excuse to not have to open the stack of mail on his desk. He locked the office and began walking north, toward Lombard Street. North Beach was alive with activity and Blake passed restaurants getting ready for the evening's diners, bars and cafes already filled with tourists, and shoppers scurrying along the sidewalks, darting from one shop to the next in search of souvenirs. He passed tourists, headed to Fisherman's Wharf and Alcatraz and the beaches.

Where Mason met Columbus, Blake continued north and looked up at Coit Tower, shining like a torch in the brilliant sunlight. A cable car, heavily laden with tourists, snaked its way toward Fisherman's Wharf, and Blake turned left onto Lombard Street. Up ahead, he could see the crooked old thoroughfare, packed with the rental cars of out-of-towners, slowly snaking their way to the hill's base. Finally, right at the foot of the hill, he found the address he had been given.

The town house, which was set up on the hill and partially obscured by overgrown shrubbery, appeared to be Art Deco in design. Blake pressed a button affixed to a gate and a buzzing sound signaled his permission to enter. He opened the gate, stepped inside, and made his way up twisting stone steps. He stopped at a red door and rapped lightly. After a few minutes, the door opened and Blake found himself standing in front of a woman in her early forties. Only about five-one, with short, blond hair, she wore white slacks, a tan, sleeveless top, and leather sandals. Her lined, leathery face suggested either stress or too many days in the sun or stress, Blake wasn't sure which, but the lines under her blue eyes hinted at fatigue.

"Ellen?"

"Mr. Danzig." She stepped aside. "Please, come in."

Blake walked into a spacious foyer. The room was tastefully decorated, with only a large mahogany table that held a flower arrangement and a single Louis XV gilt chair. A lone painting, a portrait by an eighteenth-century painter, graced the darkly paneled wall. To his left was a living room.

"Thank you for coming," Ellen said, directing Blake to the living room.

"No problem. Now, what seems to be the—"

A specter walked through the living room. She was dressed as though she had died in the 1970s, and half of her face was horribly burned.

"You have a ghost." Blake turned to Ellen. "She just walked through the room."

"Look," Ellen said, clearly agitated, "as I told you on the phone, I don't really believe in this sort of thing, but I want whatever it is gone."

Blake considered his host for a moment, then took a seat on the sofa. "What is it your ghost doing?" He was as polite as possible.

"It...she opens drawers and cupboards," Ellen stammered. "She turns on lights."

"Has she ever harmed you?"

"Mr. Danzig," Ellen's voice was icy, "I paid a great deal of money for this town house, and I do not intend to share it with a ghost."

Blake's face grew hot, but he remained silent.

"I'll pay you anything you want just get that bitch out of my house and send her wherever it is that you send them."

"We won't discuss payment until I know what needs to be done." He rose and looked in the direction the ghost had gone. "I'll need to talk to her," he said, "do you mind?"

"By all means," Ellen replied coolly, "as long as you take her with you."

Blake ignored Ellen's last comment and walked into the kitchen. Obviously the poor woman was merely under a great deal of stress. Unfortunately, he didn't see any sign of the ghost in the kitchen, so he returned to the living room.

"Well?" Ellen asked.

"She wasn't in there. May I look upstairs?"

Ellen threw her hands up in reply and Blake climbed the carpeted stairs. In a bedroom, he found the spirit rummaging through a drawer. She looked up, surprised.

"Hello," he said. "Don't be afraid. I'm here to help you."

To his amazement, the ghost smiled and sat on the edge of the bed.

❖

"Well?" Ellen asked, once Blake got back to the living room. He had been upstairs for half an hour, and Ellen seemed about to go crazy.

"She died here in nineteen sixty-nine," Blake explained, "in a fire. She doesn't mean you any harm."

"I don't give a damn. It's my house and I want her out of here."

"It was her house first, and she doesn't intend to leave it. I did make her promise to stop turning on your lights, however."

"Mr. Danzig," Ellen said, her voice rising, "I simply refuse to share my home with a…with…"

"A ghost."

"I don't give a damn what you call it. Just get rid of it."

She went to a table and, from a drawer, retrieved a pen and a checkbook. "Name your price," she said, a crazed expression on her face. "I'll pay you anything to help me."

Blake, who had already headed for the door, stopped and faced her. "I can only help these ghosts move on when they're ready. This one," he motioned to the stairs, "loves this house and is not ready to move on. I'm sorry."

"Mr. Danzig," Ellen's eyes were suddenly moist, "I'm terrified. I don't know if I can live here with a…a ghost."

"She won't harm you. But, please, call me if you need anything else."

Blake stepped out onto the walkway and strode back down the hill, leaving Ellen to deal with her ghost. As he headed home, he hoped that the ghost at the Bayside Bar was willing to move on.

CHAPTER FIFTEEN

Blake arrived at the Bayside Bar at one thirty, just in time for last call. Joe, who was serving a beer to one of the last hangers-on, grinned and waved.

"Hey," he said, leaning over the bar and kissing Blake on the lips. "You ready for some ghost-busting?"

"Ready. Anything weird happen tonight?"

"Nothing besides the usual. A couple of broken glasses, some jukebox trickery, but other than that, nothing."

As Blake turned to see clientele departing, he glimpsed the blond spirit standing beside the jukebox and leering at him. As before, he walked to the bathroom and disappeared.

This time Blake followed.

"Where are you going?" Joe asked.

"Our boy just went into the men's room."

He cautiously pushed the door open, aware the ghost was capable of inflicting harm. Instead, the spirit was propped against the wall beside the urinal. He gazed at Blake, a sad hunger lingering in his eyes.

"Why are you here?" Blake ignored the ghost's flirtations.

"Same reason you are." The spirit came across the room and stopped in front of Blake. "You're hot," he said.

"You've been following me. Why?"

The ghost smiled coyly and returned toward the urinal.

"You hurt my friend." Blake said. "That's not cool."

"The lesbian?" The ghost laughed. "What do you need with a lesbian?"

"She's a friend who happens to be a lesbian, and nobody hurts my friends."

"I'm sorry," the ghost replied, insincerely. "Don't you want to fuck me?"

"I hate to be the one to break it to you," Blake locked eyes with the ghost, "but you're dead."

The ghost looked stunned but his expression quickly changed to rage. He kicked over the metal garbage can beside the sink and flew through the door. The sounds of shattering glass in the bar brought Blake rushing out of the bathroom. The bar was empty of patrons, and Joe stood behind the bar, his shoulders slumped.

"Joe?" Blake called. "Did he hurt you?"

Joe didn't respond. Blake rounded the bar and placed a hand on his shoulder.

"Joe?"

When Joe still didn't reply, Blake gently spun him around. "Joe, did the ghost hurt you?"

Joe slowly lifted his head, but to Blake's horror, his blue eyes were black. The blackness even covered the whites of his eyes. A twisted, evil grin spread over his face. "Joe's gone," the spirit's voice said.

"Shit!" Blake pushed his possessed boyfriend back. "Get out of him, you asshole."

"Now you can make love to me, Blake," the spirit replied. "Come on…fuck me."

He attempted to put his arms around Blake's neck, but Blake pushed him away. "No. I love Joe, not you."

Joe's face contorted into the most fearsome grimace Blake had ever seen. "Fine. Then Joe can join me!"

He reached for a kitchen knife, which was lying on the bar next to the sliced fruit containers. Before Blake could comprehend what was happening, the ghost stabbed Joe in the stomach with the sharp blade.

For the first time since he became possessed, Joe spoke. "Blake," he gasped. "Help me."

Joe fell to the floor, and the ghost left Joe's body and disappeared through the back wall.

❖

Thinking quickly despite feeling he was underwater, Blake grabbed his cell phone and dialed 911.

"Please," he said, his heart pounding, "my boyfriend has been stabbed. He needs an ambulance. We're at the Bayside Bar. Hurry!"

"Who stabbed him?" the dispatcher asked.

"It...it was an attempted robbery."

"Is the attacker still there?"

"No." Blake looked down at poor Joe, a pool of blood growing under him. "Please hurry!"

Blake ended the call and dialed Brian's cell phone. "Brian," he said, grateful that he had actually answered. "I need you. I'm at the Bayside Bar, and a friend of mine has been stabbed."

"Call the police," Brian said. "I'll be right there, okay?"

Dazed, Blake called 911 again. He had just finished the call when Brian walked in. "What happened?"

"A ghost stabbed him." Blake suddenly felt dizzy. This had just proved Brian's point, right? Date Blake Danzig and you deal with all kinds of crazy, paranormal shit. Maybe even die.

Brian seemed to sense Blake's discomfort. "Blake," he said, touching Blake's shoulder tenderly, "this isn't your fault. I know that."

Blake nodded, his throat constricting and making it impossible to speak.

"Just get this bastard," Brian said, his voice low. "That's what you do, right?"

"He could die," Blake finally managed to blurt. The tears he had been trying to control began to fall. "He could die, and it's all because I've got this stupid gift. You were right to leave when you did, Brian."

"Blake, for the first time since meeting you I think I can imagine, just the smallest bit, what it must be like. And I was a coward for bolting the way I did. Me, the tough cop with a gun, afraid of ghosts. Your boyfriend, Joe," he said, gesturing to the bar, "he's the brave one. I was selfish. Joe is a better person than I could ever hope to be. Don't give up on him."

Suddenly, they embraced and held one another for a moment before Blake spoke. "Thank you," he whispered, finally releasing Brian. "Will you do me one more favor?"

"Anything."

"Look through old police reports. There has to be some sort of record of a guy in his twenties having died here. If I know who I'm dealing with, I might have a better chance of getting rid of him."

"I'll call you as soon as I know something."

The owner of the Bayside Bar, an older gay man—in his late fifties or early sixties—had come to the bar after a call from the police regarding the attack. The man, with his gray hair pulled back in a ponytail and a white beard, locked up the bar after the police departed.

He called to Blake as he walked up the street. "Mr. Danzig," he hurried to catch up, "would you like a ride somewhere?"

"I was going to catch a cab," Blake said, grateful for the company, "but sure, I'd appreciate that."

"My name's George." The man extended his hand.

"Blake," he said, shaking George's hand.

"I know who you are. I've seen your show."

Blake was in no mood to ask whether George was a fan. He just wanted to get to the hospital to see how Joe was doing.

They walked to a white, two-door Porsche parked nearby, and Blake climbed into the passenger seat.

"Where to?" George asked.

"They said they were taking Joe to St. Mary's."

George nodded and set off through the deserted streets of the sleeping city. As they drove, Blake felt very alone. Not the aloneness that everybody feels at night, cut off from the rest of the world, but truly alone. Perhaps, because of what had just happened to Joe, but also because he was afraid that Joe, like Brian, would leave him alone.

He looked at George. "Can I ask you about your bar's ghost?"

George chuckled. "You mean Charlie?"

"Yes. Why do you call him Charlie?"

"Hell, I don't know." George laughed. "I had to call it something."

"Have you ever seen it?"

"Sure. A blond kid, not bad-looking, but a real pain in the ass. Constantly breaking glasses and turning on lights."

"Do you know why he haunts your bar?"

George shook his head. "Died there, I guess. But not on my watch. I've only owned the place four years."

❖

George let Blake off at the emergency-room exit on Bush Street and handed him a business card before driving away. "Call me when they know something." His expression was stony.

Blake nodded and thanked George for the ride before walking into the hospital.

Aside from churches and cemeteries, a hospital was one of the worst places for him to be. It was literally a jumping-off point to the spirit world, and this hospital was no different from any other. Ghosts of every age, gender, and race roamed the halls and waiting rooms, either recently deceased or forever trapped within the walls of the institution. Blake did his best to not make eye contact with any of them. He had learned that once they realized he could see them they always spoke, and he was in no mood to deal with spirits, not while Joe was stuck between life and death. He gritted his teeth and walked into the waiting room.

It was more crowded than Blake would have imagined, with two people standing in line ahead of him. Fortunately, the admitting nurse, a tall, pretty brunette with dark brown eyes, was a fan of *Haunted California* and recognized Blake.

"How may I help you, Mr. Danzig?" she asked.

"A friend of mine was brought in, stabbed in an attempted robbery."

"Let's see." She consulted her computer screen. "He was admitted and taken right into surgery…"

"Is he all right?" Blake was suddenly panicked.

"It looks like he's still in surgery. If you'd like to have a seat, I'll have the doctor talk to you when he's finished."

"Thanks." Blake located an empty chair and wearily sat down. Resting his head back against the cold, white wall, he closed his eyes, hoping he could sleep. Maybe he would wake up and Joe would be okay or, better yet, he would discover this had all been a bad dream. But he was only kidding himself. The reality of the situation was probably that Joe, even if he did make it through surgery, would probably never want to see him again. And who could blame him? After all, wasn't it Blake's "gift" that caused the ghost to do what he did in the first place? Without his ability to see ghosts, there would never have been an attack and, as he drifted off, Blake wished his gift would go away.

"Mr. Danzig." Someone was shaking him. Blake opened his eyes, his neck stiff from sitting upright in the uncomfortable chair. He looked at his watch. It was four o'clock. It took him a moment to clear his head. He had been dreaming of Melody, and in the dream she had cast a magic spell on him to remove his "gift." Was that possible? He decided to ask her the next time he saw her and jumped up from his seat.

"Is he going to be all right?" Blake's voice was shaking.

"Your friend was lucky," said the doctor, a handsome young man of Arabic descent. "The knife pierced the abdominal wall but missed any major organs."

Waves of relief washed over Blake. "Can I see him?"

"I'm afraid not." The doctor looked serious. "The knife wound appeared to have been self-inflicted and your friend kept talking about being possessed. Therefore, I felt it in his best interest to have him moved to the psychiatric ward."

The doctor's words slammed into Blake like a freight train. Not only had he caused Joe to be stabbed by a malevolent ghost, but also be locked up like an insane man. Blake collapsed back into the chair, his mind reeling.

"That's crazy. He was stabbed. I was there!"

"I'm sorry, but we have to follow certain procedures in cases like this. Your input is certainly helpful, though, and I'll see what I can do."

"When can I see him?" Blake managed to say, his voice weak.

"We'll keep him under observation for twenty-four hours. After that, we'll have to wait and see."

Blake nodded dumbly, and the doctor walked away without another word.

Thoroughly exhausted, Blake was getting up when his cell phone—which was on vibrate mode—began to dance in his pocket. He pulled it out, relieved to see it was Brian. After striding out of the waiting room, he ignored the others lingering outside and hastily explained what the doctor had told him.

Brian was silent for a moment. Finally, he said, "It makes sense. But don't worry. I'll try to pull some strings and get him out of there. I mean, we have a witness to the attack. I'll just explain that he was holding the knife as he tried to fight off his attacker. That should clear things up."

"Thanks, Brian. But no matter how much you fix it, I doubt our relationship will go any further after tonight."

"Relationship?" Brian raised an eyebrow as Blake nodded. "Don't talk that way, okay? If Joe loves you, it will be fine. And I've got good news. I think I've found out who your ghost is."

"Who?"

"His name was Derek Marshall, and he was a little too

fond of cocaine. Ten years ago he overdosed in the bathroom at the bar, and he matches your description."

"Thanks." Blake hung up his phone and stepped closer to Bush Street, searching for a taxi. Whether Derek Marshall was ready to move on was irrelevant. He was dangerous and would have to, whether he liked it or not.

❖

As promised, Blake awakened George with the news of Joe's surgery. Hesitantly, he recounted the true story of what had happened at the bar and the need to deal with it.

"I always knew the place was haunted." George's voice was tired. "I called him Charlie and never thought he'd hurt anyone. Break glasses, yes. But not try to stab one of my bartenders."

Despite having been awakened twice that night, George agreed to meet Blake back at the bar. He was just getting out of his Porsche when the cab carrying Blake arrived.

"Do you mind if I come in and watch?" George asked as he unlocked the door.

Blake considered the situation. The spirit had briefly possessed Joe. Would he attempt the same thing with the owner? "I'm not sure. He's dangerous."

"Hell." George chuckled. "I've been around the block. If AIDS and gay bashers couldn't get me, then neither can any fucking ghost."

Blake considered him for a moment, then nodded. Who was he to argue with that reasoning? "Okay, but there's no shame in running if things get hairy."

They entered the bar, which George illuminated by

flipping a series of switches on a circuit breaker located behind the door. The room was oddly silent, and Blake stepped cautiously toward the bar. George, who seemed exhilarated by the experience, looked around excitedly.

"Derek," Blake called in a loud voice. "Derek Marshall. Are you still here?"

Suddenly, the jukebox behind them came to life and George—despite his earlier bravado—jumped. "Shit," he said, laughing. "Sorry, that surprised me."

The jukebox didn't faze Blake. "We're not here to listen to music, Derek. You hurt my friend and we can't let you hurt people."

The door to the men's room swung slowly open and the spirit emerged. George, who had never actually seen the spirit manifest when summoned, gasped and took a step back.

"It's time for you to move on," Blake said. "You're dead."

The ghost stopped abruptly, seeming confused.

"You overdosed in the bathroom, remember?"

"No." The spirit's voice was almost a whisper. "No."

"Yes, you're a goddamned drug addict and you killed yourself in that bathroom by shoving cocaine up your nose."

"No. That's a lie."

"Doesn't it make you feel like shit, knowing what you did to your poor mother by killing yourself like that? It's time for you to go now, Derek."

"You can't tell me what to do," the ghost shouted. Suddenly, he was standing in front of Blake, his eyes wild. "It was an accident!"

"You're dead," Blake said, undaunted. "Leave this place now."

"You can't make me leave," the ghost said, his face contorted into an evil grimace.

George stepped forward. "I can. This is my bar, and doing drugs on the premises is forbidden." Then, pointing to the door, he dropped his dreaded bombshell. "You're eighty-sixed," he yelled. "Don't ever come back here again!"

To Blake's astonishment, George had apparently said the magic words, because the ghost's expression turned to one of outrage and he stormed out the door. It slammed shut behind him with such force that a poster tumbled from the wall beside it.

"Very good," Blake said. "Maybe you should take my job." Then he looked back at the door. While it was true that the ghost had been cast from the bar, he was still out there and knew where Blake lived. He hoped he had seen the last of the psychotic spirit, but was prepared for all-out war if he reappeared.

❖

Blake went home and tried to sleep but, distraught over what had happened to Joe, tossed and turned. At ten o'clock, he got out of bed and dialed Melody's number. After he quickly explained what had happened the night before, and certain that he and Joe were finished, he announced that he had made a decision. "I want you to do a spell to take away my ability to see ghosts," he said resignedly.

"Blake—"

"Don't argue with me, Mel. I've thought it through, and the only way I'll ever have a chance at a normal relationship is to get rid of this supposed gift. I've made my mind up."

Melody's mind was racing. "Shouldn't you discuss this with your parents? What would they say?"

"They would tell me not to do it. But it isn't ruining their lives. It's ruining mine."

Melody felt like someone had knocked the breath out of her. What about the show, she wanted to ask. What about the paranormal-investigation business? But she could sense Blake's desperation, his pain, and so decided against making this about her.

"I don't know if I can magically make your powers just go away," she replied calmly. "But maybe we could do a binding spell."

"Fine," Blake replied, sounding relieved. "Do it."

"It will only work if you do it."

"All right." Blake sighed. "Can I come over and get it done?"

"Come over tonight, a little before midnight."

Melody hung up the phone and located her spell book, which contained the binding spell. With any luck, Blake would change his mind. She had, after all, managed to put away quite a bit of money. But she wasn't sure how the show's producers would feel about Blake breaking his contract, which clearly stipulated that he film a certain number of episodes per season.

CHAPTER SIXTEEN

To Melody's chagrin, Blake arrived at her apartment promptly at ten minutes to midnight, appearing tired, his normally attractive dark eyes hollow shells. He seemed to be in a trance, not really seeing or hearing anything around him.

"You're right on time," Melody said as she held the door open.

"I heard from Brian. They've moved Joe from the psychiatric ward into a regular hospital bed."

"That's great news. Did you go see him?"

"No." Blake directed his gaze to the floor. "He won't want to see me again, and I don't blame him."

"How do you know?" Melody touched his arm. "You have to talk to him."

Blake shook his head, his eyes dark. "Can we just get this…this thing out of me?"

"Blake," Melody said, changing tactics, "have you thought about what the network will say about this? You're under contract. And Marty will shit a brick."

"Fuck them. I've been a freak show since I was a kid and I'm tired of it."

Seeing she couldn't change Blake's mind, Melody walked into her bedroom.

When she didn't return, Blake realized he was meant to follow, and he walked to the bedroom door. Peering into the room, he saw that Melody had placed four pillar candles in a circle. She was lighting them as he entered the room, and she jerked her head toward the middle of it.

"Sit in the middle," she instructed him, her voice emotionless.

Blake complied and accepted a piece of paper, which had the spell written on it, along with a length of yellow cord.

"This is one of the oldest magic spells in the world," Melody explained. "You'll tie a series of nine knots in the cord, each one binding your ability to see ghosts. As you tie each knot, recite the corresponding line from the spell and picture your gift being bound."

Blake nodded. "Seems simple enough," he commented as he looked at the cord. "Almost like going to the doctor to have a tumor cut out."

"Are you sure you want to do this?"

"I'm positive."

Without another word, Melody picked up her dagger and, her back to Blake, moved around the circle, summoning what she addressed as the Guardians of the Watchtowers of the north, south, east, and west. When she finished, she turned to Blake and nodded. "You may begin," she said, solemnly.

Blake tied the first knot, visualizing his "gift" removed, and read from the piece of paper. "With knot of one, the spell's begun," he recited.

"With knot of two, the spell cometh true," he said as he tied the second knot.

He tied the third knot. "With knot of three, so mote it be."

"With knot of four, the power I store," he said, tying the fourth knot.

"With knot of five, the spell's alive."

"With knot of six, the spell I fix."

"With knot of seven, events I'll leaven," Blake read. Was it working?

He concentrated harder. No more ghosts, no more midnight whispers, but, possibly, a lasting relationship in exchange.

"With knot of eight, it will be Fate."

Blake tied the ninth and final knot, pulling the cord very tight.

"With knot of nine, what's done is mine!"

He looked up at Melody, expectantly, but she turned away and released the quarters, this time moving counter-clockwise around the circle. When she finished she began to snuff out the four candles surrounding Blake. "Do you feel any differently?" she asked, finally.

Blake thought for a moment. Something was different, but what was it? The constant chatter that surrounded him for years was gone. The whispers were gone. He jumped up and hugged Melody. "It worked!" he exclaimed, beaming. "Thank you!"

He looked at the knotted cord in his hand. "What do I do with this?" He looked from the cord to Melody.

"Put it in a safe place. If you ever want to reverse the spell, just unknot the cord in reverse."

Blake grimaced and thrust the cord at Melody. "I don't ever want to reverse that spell," he said, raising his voice. "Burn it."

"If you're sure." Melody took the cord.

"I'm sure."

"Blake," Melody softly touched his arm, "are you afraid of death?"

The question took Blake by surprise and he searched her face for any clue as to what she was getting at. "No," he said after a moment. "Why?"

She sat down on the edge of her bed and, instead of answering the question, posed another. "Why not?"

"Death is just another step in life. It's inevitable."

"But that doesn't mean you can't be frightened by it. So why aren't you afraid?"

Blake sighed and sat down on the bed next to her. "I guess it's because I know that things don't end when we leave this." He waved a hand around the room. "And I don't believe in heaven and hell, not literally anyway."

"Because of your powers. Not many human beings are as lucky as you are to know all of that."

Here it is, Blake thought. Instead of arguing, however, he kissed Melody on the cheek and took her hand. "I don't know if what I did tonight was right or wrong, but I have to try."

As soon as Blake had gone, Melody pulled a wooden box from her cupboard and carefully coiled the yellow cord inside. Blake might change his mind—at least she hoped he would—and she would protect the cord from harm for when that day came. She closed the lid and placed the box back in the cupboard, then strode into the living room. She pulled her address book from a drawer and flipped through the pages, searching for a number, a number Blake had given her in case of emergencies when he was still dating Brian. Fortunately, Brian answered on the second ring, even though it was well past midnight.

"Brian," she said, "we need to talk." Melody almost felt as if she was betraying Blake's confidence to someone she barely knew, but she didn't know what else to do. She was telling Brian how lonely Blake had been since their breakup when Brian interrupted.

"Melody," he said, impatience creeping into his voice. "I feel for Blake, I do, but what do you want me to do? I'm sorry the way things ended between me and Blake, but I can't change the past."

"I'm not talking about the past. I'm talking about the future."

"What do you mean?"

"Blake asked me to do a spell to strip him of the ability to see ghosts. We just did it tonight."

"What? Can you do that?"

"I can only bind the powers." Melody was happy to realize she had finally gotten through to Brian. "I don't know if a spell exists to get rid of that sort of thing."

"He did this for his boyfriend?"

"He did it for himself. He's convinced that he and Joe are finished because of what happened. No, he did this so he can have a chance at a normal relationship."

"Can you undo the spell?"

"It's a simple knot spell. It can be undone, but only by Blake."

"What can we do?"

"I don't know. He's set on this and wouldn't even let me try to talk him out of it."

"Let me see what I can do. I'll call you tomorrow."

"Thanks, Brian. This whole thing just feels wrong, like Blake did it for all of the wrong reasons."

For once, Brian Cox seemed to agree with a witch.

CHAPTER SEVENTEEN

After Blake left Melody's apartment he decided to walk home. It was after midnight and it would be nearly an hour before he reached Nob Hill, but Blake didn't care. He suddenly felt free of a heavy weight that he had been forced to carry his entire life, and he wanted to relish the feeling.

Not only were the whispers gone, the incessant babbling of a thousand ghostly voices, but the streets, too, seemed to be free of spirits. He would no longer pass the ghost of a dead cowboy on his way to the market or see dead prostitutes beckoning him into deserted alleys. He was free of it all.

Of course, he knew they were still there—they always would be—but he had freed himself from the ability to see and hear them. And Blake willingly embraced the old adage that ignorance is bliss.

Now, he told himself, he could meet somebody without bringing to the relationship all the baggage that came with his former "gift," and, maybe—just maybe—the relationship would last longer than a couple of months. Joe's face suddenly flashed in Blake's mind and a pang of guilt washed over him.

No, he told himself, forget Joe. It's time for a fresh start, unencumbered by the past.

Blake couldn't even begin to imagine what his mother would say when she learned he had bound his gift. He considered not telling her. After all, why should she have to know? But Blake knew all too well that she would, instinctively. In fact, she was probably leaving him a message right now.

Blake arrived in front of his building forty minutes later, perspiring mildly. He took a deep breath, inhaling the fresh sea air. Everything around him was still, blessedly still. He walked into his building, happy with the knowledge that the night would hold nothing more than a peaceful sleep.

❖

Brian hated hospitals. As a detective he was forced to visit them regularly, whether to question a victim, question a suspect, or visit a wounded fellow cop. How many times had he been in a hospital in the last two years? Twenty times? Thirty? He tried not to think of it, but his real problem with hospitals had nothing to do with his work. More likely they reminded him just how fragile life is, that one day he, too, might end up here or, worse, dead.

Joe was unsuccessfully attempting to reposition himself in his hospital bed when a handsome young cop entered the room. Joe glanced at his visitor. "Would you mind…" he said, motioning to the pillows piled behind him.

While his injury wasn't life-threatening, the wound—which had pierced his abdominal wall and resembled an appendectomy incision—made moving painful. The cop, who

Joe assumed was there to question him yet again about the stabbing, was amiable enough.

"Thanks," Joe said, settling back into his newly adjusted pillows. "I guess you're here about the attack."

"I know all about the attack. And I know that there was no real attempted robbery."

Joe felt his face flush and his heart began to beat faster. Before Joe could respond, however, the officer smiled reassuringly and sat on the edge of the bed.

"I know a ghost possessed your body and stabbed you, and I also know you recently began dating Blake Danzig."

"Who are you?" Joe asked, startled.

"My name is Brian Cox. I used to date Blake, before I got spooked by the ghosts and left him."

"Where's Blake?" Joe asked expectantly. "I haven't seen him since the night of…well…" He pointed at his stomach.

"He assumes it's over between the two of you," Brian's face was serious, "because of what happened."

The announcement stunned Joe.

"Is it over?" Brian asked.

"No." Joe's face was hot. "Why would he assume—"

"Because of assholes like me. He's gotten used to guys bailing on him as soon as the ghost thing gets too intense."

"I'm not like that," Joe said firmly. "No offense."

"None taken." Brian rose from his seat on the edge of the bed.

"The night the ghost attacked," Joe said, suddenly recalling a lost memory, "it was like I was being held under water…when it was inside of me. I can't really describe what it felt like, but I do remember Blake telling the spirit that he loved me."

Brian didn't reply.

"Anyway, knowing that is the one thing that made this whole ordeal worthwhile."

"Do you love him?"

"I think so…yes."

"I'm glad to hear that, because that's what he needs to hear, especially after what he gave up for you."

Joe stared at Brian, confused.

"His friend Melody, the witch, cast a spell on him to remove his ability to see ghosts. He asked her to, so he could have a normal relationship."

"He did that for me?" Joe was deeply touched. "I would never have asked him to do that."

"You need to tell him that, as soon as you're able to get out of here."

"You can bet on it."

❖

As he had predicted, Blake had slept soundly on his first night after performing the spell. Without his powers, no visitors awakened him from his slumber.

That night, however, free of the usual interruptions, Blake dreamed. Unfortunately, the dream was more like a nightmare, probably caused by the binding spell. In it, Blake was sitting beneath a large oak tree and, in the distance, he could see the circus of his youth. As he watched, the circus began moving farther away, sending huge columns of dust into the dry, windy air. Afraid that he would be left behind, Blake got up and ran after the departing circus, all the while shouting for his parents to wait for him. But when he caught up, neither of his parents recognized him.

"But I'm Blake," he said, looking from his mother to his father. "I'm your son."

His mother looked at him, expressionless. "This is our son." She held open the lid to a wooden box.

Blake peered inside and spied a yellow, knotted cord.

He awakened from the dream with a start, drenched in sweat, and had a difficult time falling back to sleep, his mother's words echoing in his head.

The next morning he woke determined to plunge into his ghost-free life. After initial hesitation, he phoned his producer Marty with the news. Marty's initial reaction, incredulous laughter, had taken Blake by surprise. "Marty," he said, calmly, "I'm not kidding. I'm done with ghost hunting."

"For the love of fucking God, kid, are you trying to give me a motherfucking heart attack?"

"No. I'm trying to give myself a regular life."

"What the fuck is that supposed to mean?" Marty bellowed. "If I knew what a goddamned 'regular life' was I would have one myself!"

"Marty—"

"You've obviously been working too much, kid," Marty said, surprising Blake by suddenly changing his tone. "Call me in a month and we'll talk."

Blake's news had a similar effect on Donatella, who he phoned after hanging up with Marty. She reacted as if Blake had announced he had just had a wart removed. No longer being able to speak with spirits took nothing away from his abilities as a writer. In fact, she suggested, this latest development could make for another good book, one in which America's favorite ghost hunter describes the latest chapter in his quest to finally be free of his burdensome "gift."

His mother, however, did not disappoint. She called him

just as he was ending his conversation with Donatella and, as Blake suspected, she claimed to have been visited by him in a dream the night before, asking for her help. Although, she explained, it wasn't really Blake in the dream, it was the part of Blake that he had gotten rid of…the part that saw ghosts.

"Why on earth would you do this to yourself?" Lila asked, her voice heavy.

Blake knew his mother's voice well enough to recognize that she had been crying, and he felt like a six-year-old again, in trouble for nicking the blade on one of the sword swallower's daggers. He decided not to tell her about his own dream.

"Mom," Blake said, keeping his voice calm, "I could never hope to get into a lasting relationship as long as I was still seeing and talking to ghosts. Most guys just aren't into that sort of thing. They want to marry a doctor or a lawyer, not spend the rest of their lives with a man who talks to ghosts."

Lila was silent.

"I did it so I could be happy. Don't you understand that?"

He resisted the urge to tell his mother that he had actually considered suicide, just to be free of his cursed gift, and suddenly remembered Moe, the old circus elephant. Had Moe's desperate act of escape been a suicide, his only way of escaping his miserable existence? Blake quickly pushed the unpleasant thoughts from his mind.

"How can you be happy," Lila asked, "when you've lost a part of yourself, something you were born with?"

"People born with illnesses have them cut out, and nobody faults them for that."

He realized instantly that the analogy would not work on his mother.

"Your gift is not an illness." Her voice was low.

"Then why did it always make me so unhappy?"

"Because you never met the right young man. It's that simple."

Blake was silent and could hear his mother sigh loudly.

"What will you do now?" she asked.

"I don't know. But I have enough money saved to last for a while. Besides, Donatella assures me that even this chapter in my life will make a good book."

"Take care of yourself, darling," Lila said. "I love you no matter what."

"I love you, too, Mom." Blake's heart was heavy. "Tell Dad I said hello."

Blake hung up, more confused than he had been since casting the spell. Nobody could wreck a good mood, could make him question the validity of his decisions like his mother, no matter how well-intended her comments. Was she right? Had he inadvertently banished a part of himself and, in the process, made himself into some sort of half person? And, if this was the case, what good would he be in a relationship as a half person? Afraid that he might have only made things worse in his quest for love, Blake headed for the door. He needed some fresh air.

❖

Lila Danzig walked out into the yard where Ben was weeding the garden. He looked up at her expectantly.

"My dream was correct," she said, solemnly. "Blake did a magic spell to bind his abilities."

Ben wiped the sweat from his forehead and regarded her for a moment. "It's his decision." He carefully weighed his words. "Maybe it's just a phase he's going through."

Lila nodded, seeming to consider this possibility.

"Don't worry, honey," Ben said. "Blake's a bright young man. He'll figure out the right thing to do."

Lila crouched down to kiss Ben. He had always been able to say the right words, the words that took the edge off life's difficult moments. She walked back into the house and began to absently scrub the inside of the oven, even though she had cleaned it only three days earlier. Certainly, Blake's childhood hadn't been a typical one, brought up in a circus among bearded ladies and sword swallowers, never staying in one town for more than a week. Perhaps, if he had only been able to have friends his own age, Blake would have turned out different. But for a boy with a mother who was a fortune teller and a father who was a contortionist, Lila doubted that playmates would have made much difference. And while siblings might have helped Blake's sense of self, well, that had simply been out of the question, too. Life on the road was difficult enough with one child. The idea of more children had been unthinkable, cruel, even. Had they made the right decision as parents? Surely Blake knew they loved him, he had to.

Lila rose from her kneeling position in front of the oven and a sharp, familiar pain surged through her chest. She grasped the counter for support and stood there until the pain subsided.

Six months, the doctor had told her. She knew better, though, even without consulting her crystal ball, something she never did for herself. Not that she was afraid of death. It was just that she wanted her life to unfold before her like a mystery, every day a surprise. Reading other people's futures was fine, but she preferred not to know her own. Knowing her future would have been like peeking at presents before Christmas morning.

Certain that this most recent episode had passed, she walked slowly into the living room to rest. Yes, she thought, it's coming, and soon. She only hoped that she had a chance to help Blake one last time.

CHAPTER EIGHTEEN

Blake stepped out onto the sunny sidewalk and crossed Sacramento Street. He strode confidently into Huntington Park, happy that he would not be seeing the usual spirits that frequented the area, many of them victims of the 1906 earthquake that had destroyed so many buildings there. As he passed children swinging on the park's swing set he was happy knowing that they were all alive, not one of them the morose spirit of a child who had once run in front of a bus. No, all of the people he was seeing were alive and enjoying life. He spotted an empty bench beside the famous Fountain of the Tortoises and sat down, admiring the bronze figures perched on the smooth marble. The water in the fountain gurgled and danced and occasionally sprayed him, carried by the strong wind. The fountain, adorned with bronze figures astride dolphins and, above them, tortoises, was an exact replica of one in Rome. William Crocker had purchased this copy in 1900, and his mansion was once located just across the street, the current site of Grace Cathedral.

Blake knew all this because the spirit of Mr. Crocker had told him, nearly a year ago, as he sat admiring the fountain.

Blake sighed. He would miss some things about not being

able to communicate with the dead, but if binding his ability meant the prospect of a normal life, he would survive. A familiar voice startled him, and he turned to find Joe, leaning on an aluminum cane.

"Joe," he said, quickly rising from the bench, "what are you doing here?"

"I was coming to see you and just happened to walk through the park on my way to your building."

"How are you?" Blake was suddenly filled with guilt for not having visited Joe in the hospital. The aluminum cane made him look even more pitiful.

"I'm fine." Joe slowly lowered himself onto the park bench. "The doctor says this should heal fairly quickly. And the cane," he said, which Blake was staring at, "I'm only using it because I'm not supposed to put a lot of weight on my leg."

Blake sat down and stared at his hands, waiting for the bombshell, the reason for Joe's visit.

"Brian came to see me at the hospital and told me a very interesting story."

"Yeah?" What the hell had Brian been up to?

"Yeah. He said you thought I wouldn't want to see you after what happened, that you assumed we were finished. Is that true?" Joe had locked Blake in his gaze, his eyes serious and sad.

"Joe." Blake's voice was beginning to quiver. "I wouldn't blame you at all if you—"

"What?" Joe's voice was firm but tender. "Deserted you? Blake, you didn't stab me, the ghost did. I was there, remember?"

"Everyone else seems to leave when the ghost thing gets a little too uncomfortable. I assumed…"

"That I was like everyone else. Well, I'm not. Listen, Blake," Joe took Blake's hand, "that night you told the ghost that you loved me. I love you, too."

Tears stung Blake's eyes and they embraced.

"I'm sorry," Blake said. "I'm yours if you still want me."

"I do. Brian told me something else."

"What?" Blake searched Joe's handsome face for a clue.

"That you did some kind of spell to get rid of your powers. Please tell me that isn't true. I would never have asked you to do that, never."

Blake was suddenly irritated with Melody, knowing that she must have called Brian.

"It's true. I'm glad to hear you say what you did, but it's done."

Joe sighed and squeezed Blake's hand. "I hope you did the right thing."

"I did. Now we can have a normal life together without worrying about ghosts, I promise."

"Want to see my scar?" Joe wagged his eyebrows conspiratorially.

"I'd love to. But are you able to—"

"No major physical exertion," Joe said, as if reciting instructions, "but I'm sure we can come up with something."

As they walked back to Blake's apartment hand in hand, Blake couldn't believe his luck. How could he have misjudged Joe so totally? He vowed that, from now on, he would do everything possible to be the best boyfriend in the world.

Upstairs, in the privacy of Blake's condominium, they kissed passionately, each hungry for the other after their days apart. Carefully, Blake pulled Joe's T-shirt off and stopped when he saw the top of a white bandage peeking over the waistband of his jeans. Blake crouched, resting on his knees, and softly kissed the bandage. Joe unbuttoned his jeans and let them slip down his legs and pulled the front of his briefs down, revealing the entire bandage.

Blake looked up at Joe's face, but Joe smiled back at him, as if apologizing for his changed appearance. With great care, Joe peeled the white surgical tape away from the bandage, exposing the ugly gash that marred his otherwise flawless abdomen. Blake was surprised at how small the incision was, and how quickly it seemed to be healing, even if the skin was still red and swollen.

"Does it hurt?" he asked.

"A little, especially when I have to use my abdominal muscles, like when I get out of bed."

Blake kissed the wound lightly, then kissed Joe's pubic hairs, which were poking over the top of his lowered underwear. Joe's cock stirred, and Blake pulled Joe's underwear down to his ankles and began to kiss the swollen cock. He suddenly stopped, looked up at Joe, and whispered, "I promise to be gentle."

❖

The next day, Blake awoke early, determined to serve Joe breakfast in bed. He was careful not to disturb him as he slipped into a robe and made his way into the kitchen.

The night before, Blake had convinced Joe he should stay at the Nob Hill condo while he was recovering. After that, they would see where things led, although Blake hoped the arrangement would become permanent.

Blake was retrieving a carton of eggs from the refrigerator when the phone rang, and he ran to grab it, not wanting to bother Joe. He was sure it was Melody, and he had a few things to tell her, anyway. Without looking at the caller ID, he said, "Hello, Melody."

"Hello, son." His father sounded tired and broken.

CHAPTER NINETEEN

The sudden death of his mother was more than Blake could bear, especially in light of their last conversation. She had passed quietly in her sleep the night before, but all Blake could think of was their last conversation and how he had disappointed her, how he had bound his powers despite her protests. If only he had visited more. He cursed himself for all the years they had missed together and worried that, somehow, over time he would forget what she looked like. And now, without his ability to talk to ghosts, he would never see her again.

"I didn't even know she was sick," Blake sobbed into the phone. "Why didn't you tell me, Dad?"

"She didn't want to worry you."

"How long did you know?"

"For over a year. She wanted it this way…no hospital, no drugs. She wanted to be here at home."

"She seemed so well during my visit." Blake collapsed heavily onto the sofa.

"You know how your mom was." Ben sounded weary, and Blake felt instantly guilty for not having been there, for not being there with his father.

"I'll get the first flight down that I can. I love you, Dad."

Blake ended the call and looked around the apartment, at everything he had amassed since moving in there. What did any of it matter now that his mother had died? He still had so much to tell her, so many questions he wished he had asked. For the first time since that night at Melody's apartment, he wished he had his powers back. Reluctantly, he dialed Melody's number and told her the news.

"Blake. I'm so sorry."

"Thanks, Mel. Can you watch things around the office while I'm gone?"

"Of course. My vacation's over anyway. You go and take as long as you need. Everything will be fine here."

Blake was silent, his heart in his throat. Why couldn't he ask?

"Blake? Are you okay?"

"I...I wish I hadn't given up my powers," he finally managed, "especially right now."

"Do you mean that?"

"Yes. I was stupid, and Joe doesn't even mind that I can see and talk to ghosts."

"I'll be right over."

She hung up the phone, leaving Blake confounded. He looked at the clock on the wall and walked into the bedroom to share the bad news with Joe.

❖

Hurriedly explaining the morning's events to Hope, Melody quickly dressed and retrieved the wooden box containing Blake's cord from the cupboard. She arrived at

Blake's condo twenty minutes later and found Blake and Joe in the kitchen. Joe was drinking coffee, while Blake spoke on the telephone with an airline ticket agent. Joe smiled feebly as she entered.

"Hi," she whispered, "nice to see you again, Joe."

"You, too."

"Hey," Blake said after he got off the phone. "Thanks for coming over."

He and Melody embraced and she placed her backpack on the counter.

"I'm flying down tomorrow morning. Joe's going to stay here. Would you mind checking in on him?"

"Not at all."

"I'll be fine."

"You're recuperating," Blake said. "I just want to make sure you're okay."

"Okay, I give up. It'll give me a chance to get to know Melody a little better."

"Blake," Melody said, looking serious, "did you mean what you said on the phone? About wishing you hadn't done the spell to bind your powers?"

Blake nodded and sat down at a counter stool. "If I still had my powers, I'd be able to see my mom again. And it turns out I was completely wrong about Joe."

Joe squeezed Blake's hand across the marble counter.

Melody pulled a wooden box from her backpack and handed it to Blake, who looked puzzled. Carefully, he opened the hinged box and discovered his knotted cord, then looked up at her.

"I thought I told you to burn this," he teased her. "Thanks for not listening to me."

"You're welcome."

"Does this mean you can get your powers back?" Joe asked.

Blake looked at Melody.

"Knot spells are the easiest to reverse," she explained. "Just untie each knot in the reverse order they were tied in and, with each knot, wish your powers back."

Blake carried the box into the living room, placed it on the coffee table, and carefully extracted the yellow cord. He looked up at Melody as she entered the room, followed by Joe.

"Do you need to do your circle thing again?" he asked.

"No, not for this."

He shifted his gaze to Joe. "Are you sure you're okay with this?"

Joe sat down next to Blake on the sofa. "I told you I love you for who you are, and I meant it."

Blake kissed Joe on the lips. "Thanks, Joe."

Then, with his friends watching, Blake unraveled the cord, wishing his powers back with each opened knot. The way the familiar whispers once again filled the room was almost comforting.

❖

The flight to Albuquerque was a fast one, and this time Ben was waiting for his son at the gate. They embraced and Ben held Blake tight for a moment before releasing him.

"Are you okay, Dad?"

Ben nodded, then sniffed. "I'm fine." He took Blake's bag, despite his protests. "How about you?"

"I'm good," Blake said. "Dad, I had Melody reverse the spell we did. I have my powers back."

"Your mother will be glad to hear that."

"What?" Blake looked slightly taken aback. "What do you mean?"

Ben smiled at him. "I can't see her, of course," he said, "but she's there at the house. I can sense her. And I have a feeling she's been waiting for you to arrive."

His father's house seemed gloomier than he remembered from his last visit. Blake noted, too, the effect on his prized garden. The plants that had once dripped over the sides of hanging baskets were now brown and lifeless. The vegetable garden, once so abundant, was now weedy, and vegetables were rotting on the vine. The once-impressive wildflowers were the only plants that seemed to have survived, but even they looked tawdry now, thick and overgrown and extending over their once clearly marked boundaries. Even the koi in the pond seemed to be in mourning and floated listlessly in the water. This sudden decay, almost overnight, surprised Blake. It was as if his mother had managed to take the life out of the house when she left. There was so much he wanted to ask her when the time came.

The wind chimes in the yard were silent as they pulled up in front of the house but, fortunately, Blake glimpsed the little girl, Jacqueline, skipping through the yard. She disappeared when she reached the next house.

For the first time in his life, Blake felt happy, blessed even, with his gift. Though he had fought it for years, something about seeing spirits comforted Blake, as if their mere existence proved there was more to life than was obvious at first. Not that Blake believed in an all-knowing God—not in the Christian sense anyway—any more than he believed in a heaven or a hell. All he knew for a certainty was that there was definitely life after death. He had to be helping the spirits cross over to someplace, right? He simply didn't believe that they were being sent to any place that the human mind could really comprehend. Blake figured he would discover what that meant specifically once he had died himself.

He had been a fool to think that he could separate that part of himself, he now realized, and he was grateful that he had been given a second chance.

"Come on," Ben said. "Your mother's waiting."

The cat, Dexter, meowed at them as they entered the house, and Blake stared sadly at his mother's crystal ball, which rested on its table by the window.

"I don't know what to do with her things," Ben said, following Blake's eyes. "I don't feel right putting them away… not yet."

A sound on the stairs caused Blake to turn and there, descending the stairs, was the spirit of Lila Danzig.

"Mom's here," Blake said.

"I told you. Tell her I miss her."

"Tell him I know that," Lila replied. Blake repeated her words to his father.

"And ask her where she put my reading glasses."

"Tell your father that they're in the drawer beside the bed where he left them."

Blake repeated this information and laughed. "This is crazy. I feel like you two are arguing and I'm stuck in the middle."

Ben patted him on the back and said, "You're right. I'll go tinker around in the yard. You two talk."

As Ben walked outside, Blake turned back to his mother's spirit. "Why didn't you tell me you were sick? I would have been around more often."

"You were so busy. I didn't want to trouble you over something that was inevitable."

"But I'm your son."

"And I'll always be your mother. And, by the way, when did you regain your abilities?"

"Yesterday. Melody helped me reverse the spell."

Lila laughed. "Your father said you would make the right decision. I suppose he knows what he's talking about every now and then."

"Actually, I only did it so I could see you again. But now that it's done, I'm glad to have my gift back."

Dexter meowed loudly at Lila's spirit from a windowsill in the living room.

"Dexter," Lila scolded him, "you have plenty of food, you bad cat."

"I'll bet poor Dexter doesn't know what to make of this."

"He doesn't," Lila said, "but he knows something has changed."

The fact that animals and children were far more capable of seeing spirits than most adults had always intrigued Blake. Perhaps it was their sense of innocence, or the fact that they simply allowed themselves to believe that imbued them with the power. But why, as adults, most people simply stopped believing puzzled Blake. It was as if, upon reaching a certain age, a switch was flipped in people's heads and faith in anything supernatural was suddenly gone, along with Santa Claus and the Easter Bunny.

"Your memorial service is tomorrow," Blake said, turning back to Lila. "Are you going?"

"Are you serious?" Lila looked scandalized. "Of course I'm going! I want to hear what people say about me. At least I had the common sense to be cremated. I hate it when people comment on how good a dead body looks."

"I saw the little girl's spirit," Blake changed the subject, "the one you called Jacqueline."

"She's a dear, but she won't leave me alone since I...well, since I passed. She thinks she's gotten a new playmate."

"Mom," Blake said softly. "I'm glad to see you, but do you think you'll hang around here? I mean, will I ever be able to see you again?"

"Remember what I taught you. If you want to contact spirits, Halloween is the easiest time to do it. But I'm sure I'll be checking in on you and your father from time to time."

"I hope so," Blake said.

❖

The small gathering at Lila Danzig's memorial service comprised mostly neighbors from their street. Sadly, none of the old circus crowd had come because, as Ben explained, after the circus was disbanded, everyone "scattered to the winds." As she had promised, Lila hovered around those in attendance, eavesdropping on their conversations. Blake did his best not to laugh at his mother's shenanigans, even when she sat in the back row, commenting loudly on the platitudes that the officiating minister offered. After the service, Lila approached Blake.

"I'm not coming home with you and your father," she

said. "I want to go see some people. But tell your father I'll check in on him soon."

"I will," Blake replied, keeping his voice low. "I love you, Mom."

"I love you, too, darling."

The spirit of Lila Danzig suddenly faded into a mist and disappeared.

❖

Neither Ben nor Blake spoke during the drive home. Lila's ashes were in an urn in Blake's lap, and the marble felt cold in his hands, but he felt oddly serene, happy almost. This, he thought, is why his mother had always referred to his ability to see ghosts as a gift. What else would you call being able to speak to your recently deceased parent? It was an ability that few other people had the privilege of claiming, and it was one that Blake vowed never to part with again. Ben, on the other hand, seemed lost deep in thought. Blake turned to his father.

"Dad," he said, "are you all right?"

Ben smiled sadly, never taking his eyes off the road. "I need to tell you something, Blake, something I promised your mother I would never do. But you have a right to know."

Blake stared at his father, speechless.

"I met your mother twenty-nine years ago when the circus—back then run by my father—was swinging down through a Mexican border town."

Blake nodded. He had heard this story before. They met, Ben's father didn't like Lila for some reason, and Ben had threatened to leave the circus unless they could be married, and so they were, shortly thereafter.

"Your mother was pregnant when I met her. That's why my father didn't approve of our marriage."

Blake stared at his father. If they had met twenty-nine years ago, the baby she was carrying had to have been Blake.

"I promised Lila I would raise you as my own son, which I am proud to say I did," Ben said. "And I have always been very proud of you."

"Who…" Blake found it difficult to speak. "Who was my father?"

"Some boy from her village."

"Why are you telling me this now?" Blake's mind was reeling under the weight of the news. It was almost as if he had suddenly lost both parents at once.

"Your mother is gone," Ben said. "I felt it was your right to know the truth, so that if you wanted to, you could go find your real father."

"You're my real father," Blake said firmly. "And I'll always love you."

Ben's eyes grew moist. "I was hoping you'd say that."

That night, as they dined at the kitchen table, Blake turned to his father. "Would you ever consider moving to San Francisco? We would at least be able to see each other more often."

Ben laughed and shook his head. "San Francisco is too big. I'm staying right here. But thank you for the thought."

"But, Dad, this house is so big and I'm worried that you'll be lonely."

"Son, I'd be lonely in San Francisco, too. A person doesn't

share their life with another for as long as your mother and I did and not feel a sense of loss."

Blake was silent, not wanting to interrupt his father.

"Love is a gift, and when it's offered to you, you'd better take it. Your mother and I had a huge hurdle to jump when we first met, namely an unexpected baby, but we loved each other and made it work. It wasn't always easy, but we shared a wonderful life and I'm eternally grateful for that."

Blake grasped his father's hand.

"Anyway, I'll be fine. At least I have Dexter and my garden...what's left of it...to keep me company. And I promise to come up to San Francisco for a visit."

"I'll hold you to that."

Blake sent his father into the living room to watch television and began gathering the dirty dishes from the table. As he washed them, he thought about what his father had said about accepting love when it's offered. Suddenly, he grabbed his cell phone and dialed Joe's number.

"Hi," Joe said, "how are you holding up?"

"Fine, just doing some dishes."

"I can't wait for you to be back in San Francisco."

"Me either. In fact, I'm calling because I want to ask you to move in with me...for good."

CHAPTER TWENTY

The next morning Blake hugged his father good-bye at the airline gate. "You promise you'll come up to visit," he said, "and that you'll call me whenever you need anything."

"I'll be fine. And, yes, I promise I'll plan a trip to San Francisco."

"I'll pay for your ticket. You just say when."

"Go, before you miss your flight." Ben hugged him again.

The cab ride from the airport to Nob Hill was a quick one, and Blake paid the fare and hurried up to his condo, eager to see Joe. When he entered his apartment he placed his bag on the floor and discovered Joe on the small balcony, enjoying a cup of coffee. He was freshly showered and wearing nothing but a pair of red athletic shorts.

Joe smiled as Blake stepped out onto the balcony. "Welcome home." He rose and kissed Blake passionately on the mouth, apparently hungry for his man after three days apart.

"Is it your home, too?" Blake asked as he gazed into Joe's eyes.

Joe lowered his head for a moment, then looked back into

Blake's eyes. "I hope so," he said. "I'm just not sure that right now is the best time."

Blake held on to Joe, afraid of what was coming next.

"Blake," Joe gripped Blake tight, "I'm not saying no. I just think we need to take things slowly. We haven't known each other that long and there are practical considerations to take into account."

"Like what?" Blake felt like a balloon that had just been deflated. "Don't you love me?"

"You know I love you. I would have to break the lease on my apartment to move in here, and I'm not sure I should do that."

"It doesn't matter," Blake said. "I own this condo—"

"And what if, for some reason, things don't work out between us? Then I'm stuck looking for another apartment with a history of having broken a lease."

Blake nodded, feeling defeated. He hated to admit it, but Joe's reasoning was sound and he could offer no further argument. "You sure gave it a lot of thought," he said, finally.

"Because I love the idea. And I hope you'll keep the offer on the table while we get to know one another a little better. Besides," he added with an extra squeeze, "my lease is up in two months."

Blake's mood lightened. Two months wasn't that long to wait.

"Come on," Joe said, leading Blake into the living room and toward the bedroom, "let me show you how much I missed you."

❖

The next day, Blake called Marty with the welcome news that he had decided not to quit the show after all. The producer sounded relieved, his tone conciliatory.

"That's good news, kid," he said. "I knew you'd make the right decision."

"When's our next taping?" Blake asked, flipping through his appointment book.

"Next Wednesday. Unless that's too soon for you. We can reschedule if you want."

Blake had to laugh at Marty's willingness to be so accommodating. Obviously Blake's threat to leave the show had put the fear of God into him.

"No, that's fine." Blake marked the date in his appointment book. "Where are we filming?"

"Alcatraz, right out your back door. A piece of cake."

"Marty, a lot of other ghost shows have already covered Alcatraz. Is it really important that we do it, too?"

"That's the point, Blake. Everybody's done it but us. We have to do it, too."

"You're right," Blake said. "Alcatraz it is, then."

❖

The following Wednesday, accompanied by Marty, Melody, and a cameraman, Blake took a ferry from Fisherman's Wharf destined for Alcatraz. The ferry, chartered solely for the *Haunted California* crew, was devoid of the groups of tourists it would usually carry to the island. As they stood on the deck, seagulls hovered just above them, riding the strong sea winds. As the massive ferry churned slowly across the bay, Blake took in the surroundings. To the east he could see the Bay Bridge, already congested with traffic headed into and out of the city. To the west was the Golden Gate, its topmost parts shrouded in patches of early fog, like bits of down, slowly creeping into the inner bay. Just past Alcatraz lay Angel Island and, past that, Sausalito.

As the ferry neared the sandstone island, Melody pointed to movement on the rocky shores. "Pelicans!" she exclaimed, snapping a photo of the ridiculous-looking birds.

"They're where Alcatraz got its name," Blake said. "*La Isla de los Alcatraces*...the island of pelicans."

"Somebody did his homework," Melody said.

Blake ignored her and watched as the pelicans suddenly took to the air. He was slightly jealous of her and her news that she and Hope had decided to move in together. He was happy for her, of course. Melody deserved to be happy and things seemed to be going well for her and her new girlfriend. Blake only wished that things would go as well for him and Joe.

The ferry circled to the east of Alcatraz and pulled up to a jetty on the north of the island, its propellers churning up the gray waters of the bay as it slowed to position itself at the point of debarkation. Blake looked up at the decaying structures looming on the horizon, their concrete walls crumbling from years of exposure to the sea air. Some of the buildings were mere shells, having been destroyed by mysterious fires in the late seventies, after the island had been closed as a prison. The main building, a massive structure at the center of the island, seemed dark and foreboding, despite the clear, sunny day. Not surprisingly, Blake became suddenly aware of voices—possibly hundreds of them—echoing from within the walls of the structure. Blake shared this information with his companions.

"I'll bet the place is full of ghosts," Melody said.

"Well, let's just remember," Blake said, recalling the ghost at the Bayside Bar, "most of these men weren't exactly law-abiding citizens when they were alive. They might not welcome us very graciously."

As they stepped off the ferry a ranger from the National Park Service, a tall, handsome young man with dark sideburns that extended down his face from under his ranger hat, greeted them. He stuck out his hand in greeting and Blake admired his tan, muscular forearms. Back in the old days, the days before Joe, the handsome ranger was the type of guy Blake would have been all over. Before the end of shooting the old Blake would have had the cute ranger bent over a bathroom sink, his pants around his ankles, getting fucked up the ass.

Get a grip, Blake told himself, *you're in a relationship now.*

Introductions were made and as the ranger, who identified himself as Craig, led them up a paved driveway and into the main prison building, Blake stole another glance at Craig's shapely ass. As Blake entered the building, the voices he had heard from outside suddenly stopped.

"That's weird," he whispered to Melody. "The voices stopped the minute I walked in."

Melody closed her eyes and breathed deeply. "They know you have the power to see them," she said. "You're like a paranormal parole board."

"That should make for a fun evening," Blake deadpanned.

In an area that the park ranger identified as the Block C utility corridor, Blake spotted numerous spirits. He mentioned this to the ranger.

"There was a prison riot here back in the mid nineteen forties," he replied. "Prisoners were killed here. Some guards were murdered, too."

Similar scenes accosted Blake in the hospital ward, the therapy room, and Cell Blocks A and B. When they reached the area known as "the hole," however, the energy was almost oppressive.

"This is where rebellious prisoners were placed for punishment," the ranger explained. "There wouldn't be a lot of happy memories attached to this area."

As they moved past the darkened, windowless cells Blake stopped in front of Cell 14-D, aware of sobbing inside. He hesitated and shared a startled expression with Melody, who also appeared to have sensed something inside. Slowly, he grasped the cold metal handle in his hand. It was rusty, its paint cracked and peeling, and was difficult to turn. With a great heave, Blake tugged and the heavy door creaked open on its rusted hinges. Inside, crouching in a far corner, was the ghost of a young man, probably only in his thirties. He was completely naked, and his pallid skin was dirty and bruised. He looked at Blake with real fear and covered his head with his hands. "Don't hurt me, sir," he whispered. "I promise not to fight anymore."

Blake took a deep breath and stepped into the cold cell. Immediately, he was overcome with great sadness and, despite the fairly warm day, he shivered. "What's your name?" he asked softly. His breath fogged the air in front of his face as he spoke.

"Sam," the ghost replied. "Sam Willis."

"Sam," Blake said, stepping aside, "you're free to go now."

"B-back to my cell?" the spirit asked.

"No. From this prison."

The spirit looked momentarily perplexed. Then, seeing that Blake was serious, he rose from the corner and slowly stepped out into the corridor, light from the high windows illuminating his pale body.

The cameraman, who was filming everything, recorded a bright orb exiting the cell. "This is good footage," he whispered to Marty, who was standing beside him.

Finally realizing his freedom was no joke, the spirit began to slowly fade and floated to the high windows. Without looking back, he disappeared through the mesh-filled glass.

The symbolism of having freed an erstwhile prisoner's ghost from a prison—both literally and figuratively—wasn't lost on Blake and, for the second time since regaining his powers, he was thankful for the opportunity to be useful. In fact, the painful realization that he had nearly locked away his own spiritual energy in a prison of his own making suddenly hit him, and Blake knew what he had to do. It was the right thing, the honorable thing, and it was his destiny.

"Come on," he said to those gathered around him. He strode purposefully out of the hole and into the main cell block. Standing at the end of the cells, he called out in a loud voice. "This prison is officially closed." His voice echoed off the cold walls and down the empty corridors. "If any of you wish to leave, you are free to do so now!"

Craig, the park ranger, touched Blake's arm. "Wait," he whispered, "I have an idea." He walked to the wall and pressed a button on an old but still functioning control panel. Suddenly, the grating sound of cell doors sliding open reverberated throughout the chamber. The group stood silent, awaiting any sign of activity. Then, slowly, spirits began to emerge from their cells.

"Wow," whispered the cameraman, whose camera recorded a mixture of orbs, mists, and shadowy figures emerging from cells, walls, and even the concrete floor.

Blake spoke once again, in a loud voice. "You're free to leave this island. Go in peace."

The spirits seemed to date back to the very beginning of the island's use as a fort and prison. Blake watched as the ghosts, a mixture of Native Americans, Civil War soldiers, and 1930s gangsters, all stepped out into the open. Even ghosts dressed in the uniforms of the former prison guards were present, and they all took Blake's cue and began to vanish, floating out the massive windows and disappearing into the night. They had been murdered, committed suicide, and died of illness and insanity. Some, Blake knew, had murdered other people during their lifetimes, but none of that mattered to him. He was no judge, was not there to damn anyone, merely there to set the spirits free of their earthly bonds.

Once the spirit activity seemed to have ceased, Marty looked at Blake. "Is that it?" he whispered. "We've filmed a lot of creepy shit over the years, but this was the most impressive display I've ever seen."

"There are still spirits here," Melody said. "I can sense them."

Blake nodded. "I can, too. They're the ones who either don't trust us or don't want to leave." He turned to Craig, the park ranger. "They may never leave."

❖

The return voyage to Fisherman's Wharf was mostly uneventful, except for a couple of enterprising spirits recently freed from Alcatraz, who took advantage of the ferry by stowing away for the short ride to the city. Apparently, it was the only way they knew to get off the island, but Blake avoided the urge to correct them. Who knew? Maybe this was how they felt they were supposed to have left Alcatraz.

Blake glanced to his right and admired the Golden Gate Bridge, now illuminated with artificial lights. Since moving to San Francisco he had been unable to cross the span without seeing numerous ghosts milling around on its deck. That had always made sense to Blake, who assumed they were the ghosts of suicides, jumpers from the bridge. It had never occurred to him, though, that the bridge might be a great setting for one of their shows. Blake realized that obtaining the necessary permits to close the bridge to traffic, however, might prove prohibitive, but he made a mental note to ask Marty as soon as they were back on shore. As Blake stood on the deck of the ferry admiring first the bridge and then the lights of the city against the dark sky, Marty approached him.

"Still sorry we did the Alcatraz thing?" he asked, grinning.

Marty was gloating but had been right, so he deserved to gloat a little.

"No," Blake admitted good-naturedly. "You were right and I feel like I helped a lot of sad spirits move on today."

Marty slapped Blake on the shoulder, a comradely gesture obviously meant to instill in Blake a sense of "no hard feelings."

"The network big shots are going to love the footage we got tonight," Marty said. "I have a feeling they'll want to sign you on for another season."

Marty studied Blake's face, seemingly for any sort of reaction, but Blake kept his eyes on the approaching skyline. "I'm on board for that," he finally said. "Honestly, Marty, I'm fine, and ready to get back to work. What we did today only made me realize that more."

"Glad to hear it, kid," he said.

"Listen, Marty," Blake said, happy to change topics, "I was wondering what it would be like to film a segment on the Golden Gate. I mean, it's filled with ghosts."

Marty turned and looked at the bridge, which was slowly receding into the distance, his expression all business.

"Hell," he said, the wheels obviously slowly turning in his head. "Permits alone will cost us a pretty fucking penny... and that's if city hall will even grant us permission to close the bridge to film."

"I thought of that."

"A lot of commuters will be pissed too. But it's not like the bridge has never been closed for filming before. And think of the publicity."

He faced Blake with a large smile. "Now that's the kind of shit I'm talking about!" He slapped Blake on the back again. "I'll talk to a buddy of mine down at city hall tomorrow and see if we can't get the ball rolling."

He abruptly turned and walked toward Melody, who was standing nearby. Probably to give her the same spiel about another season, Blake guessed.

Once back at the wharf, they went their separate ways, all but Blake and Melody, who hailed a cab.

"First stop, Mason and Sacramento," Blake instructed the driver, "then to the Mission."

As the cab pulled away from the curb, Blake turned to Melody. "So I guess you got the same talk from Marty?"

"About another season? Yeah. I told him I was in if you were. He said you were."

Blake nodded. "It felt good…what we did today. I suppose that's what I was meant to do with my life."

"I'm in for it as long as you are." Melody took his hand. "I really am glad we met."

Blake looked at her, filled with what could only be described as love. "Mel, I…"

"I love you, too," she said softly.

The cab slowed at the top of Sacramento Street. "Where do you want to get out?" the driver asked, looking in the mirror.

"Right here's fine." Blake fished enough money from his pocket to cover Melody's fare, too, and thanked the driver. "Tell the wife I said hello," he said to Melody as he exited the cab.

As the cab drove away toward the Mission, Blake walked the remaining few steps to his building and got on the elevator. As he stepped into his apartment, pleasant smells emanating from the kitchen greeted him. Joe stepped out of the kitchen wearing nothing but an apron, and Blake grinned.

They might not officially be living together yet, but playing house was going to be fun.

CHAPTER TWENTY-ONE

Two weeks later, the ringing telephone beside the bed woke Blake from a sound sleep. Still naked from their earlier lovemaking, Joe rolled over and grimaced at Blake. "Who the hell could that be?" he grumbled before quickly dozing off again.

Blake looked at the alarm clock on the bedside table. It was five in the morning and Joe hadn't gotten off work from his shift at the Bayside Bar until after two. Although he was perturbed at the ridiculous hour, Blake answered, not recognizing the number and aware that somebody could be in trouble. He hoped it wasn't his father.

"Hello?" he whispered into the receiver, concerned.

"Blake? Blake Danzig?"

The English accent told him right away that it was Clive Damon on the other end of the line. Blake was suddenly both relieved and irritated. Relieved because it wasn't the police calling to say that someone he loved was lying in the morgue but irritated that Clive had disturbed him at such an early hour. He collapsed back onto his pillow with the receiver still to his ear. He did his best to not sound irate.

"Clive." He sighed. "It's five o'clock in the morning here. Is everything all right?"

"Yes, of course," Clive replied cordially. "Sorry. I forgot about the time difference. It's one in the afternoon here… tomorrow, or whatever it is."

He forced a laugh that made Blake want to hang up.

"What can I do for you, Clive?" Blake asked evenly. He looked over at Joe, who had fortunately fallen back to sleep.

"Well, you see, it's just that I plan to be in your neck of the woods this weekend and was hoping that we could have dinner."

"Clive, I'm seeing someone now. I don't think that that would be a good idea."

Clive laughed again, but, this time, his laugh was haughty and dismissive. "Dear boy. I am not proposing anything untoward. I simply wish to discuss a business proposal with you. Bring along your new love, if you like, and your charming co-host. Melody, isn't it?"

"You should talk to my agent about that sort of thing—"

"Nonsense," Clive drawled. "Either I talk to you or I talk to no one. There are plenty of other paranormal shows I can approach."

"But our two are the best," Blake replied dryly.

"Precisely. What do you say?"

"All right. When do you arrive?"

❖

Despite her vehement dislike for Clive Damon, Blake was able to convince Melody to accompany him to dine with the Englishman. Her one condition was that she be allowed to bring Hope, and Blake readily agreed. "The more sane people present, the better," he joked.

Her bluff called, Melody had no option other than to attend the dinner, which Blake had booked at the restaurant atop the St. Francis Hotel on Union Square. Being the closest two to the hotel, Blake and Joe arrived first, followed quickly by Melody and Hope, who was in uniform. Melody, on the other hand, wore a strapless black cocktail dress and patent-leather high heels.

"You look terrific," Blake said, pulling a chair out for Melody.

"I feel like Jodie Foster at the Academy Awards," she grumbled as she took her seat.

"Sorry about the uniform," Hope said. "I have to go to work after dinner."

"You look great, too," Blake replied.

Melody looked around. "So where's His Lordship?"

Just then, there was a commotion at the door and they turned to see Clive, signing autographs for two starstruck women. Blake stood and motioned to him, and he approached the table with a wide smile.

"Blake Danzig!" he called as he approached.

Melody rolled her eyes, which made Joe laugh.

"Hello, Clive." Blake cast an evil look at Melody. "Please, have a seat."

As Clive sat between Hope and Joe, Blake made introductions.

"It's comforting to see that we have an officer of the law present," Clive said when he met Hope. "And, of course, I am familiar with Melody."

When Blake introduced Joe, however, Clive's face twisted into a mischievous grin. "So," he said, gripping Joe's hand tight, "you're Blake's new love."

"I'm very pleased to meet you," Joe replied. "I'm a big fan of your show."

"Thank you," Clive said. "I truly appreciate my many, many fans. Tell me, Joe, what is your profession?"

"Um, I actually have two jobs," Joe, reddening. "I'm a waiter at a restaurant here in San Francisco and I bartend part-time."

"How charming," Clive winked at Blake, "a real food-service professional."

His obvious condescension infuriated Blake but he held his tongue. He tried to ignore Clive's dig and picked up the menu on the table in front of him. "Why don't we order appetizers?"

The majority of the dinner conversation was provided courtesy of Clive, who talked endlessly of his paranormal experiences and the inherent dangers involved in the undertaking of ghost hunting.

"Most lay people," Clive said, directing his gaze at Joe, "simply do not understand what is involved when you come face-to-face with a spirit."

He was on his fourth martini, and Blake could see that it was beginning to have an effect on him. With any luck he would pass out.

"Which is what brings me to my proposal, which I briefly mentioned in Albuqueque. I have given it a lot of serious thought since then and wanted to reassure you that I am serious about it," Clive pronounced. "Only you, Blake, are as experienced as I in the field of paranormal research, which is why I think we should combine forces."

"What exactly do you have in mind?" Blake asked. His head was beginning to hurt from Clive's incessant bragging, and he touched Joe's leg under the tablecloth. All he really wanted to do was to go home and fuck Joe's brains out, not sit and listen to this fraud's endless self-glorification.

"I propose," Clive said, pausing for dramatic effect, "that we create one program by combining our two. We would share staff and resources and call it...I don't know...*Haunted Planet*...or something of the sort."

"Like I said on the phone," Blake replied, "that isn't a decision I can make on my own. You need to contact Marty or Donatella."

"You seemed rather interested in the idea in New Mexico," Clive snapped, his voice suddenly slurred. "Or was that just when we were together in my hotel room?"

Melody, who had been quiet through most of the meal, dropped her fork, which clattered on her plate. She stared disbelievingly at Blake. "Are you serious?" she asked, looking scandalized. "You said you two just had a couple of drinks."

"And then a bit more 'refreshment,'" Clive said, looking from Melody to Blake and licking his lips lasciviously. He turned his icy stare to Joe. "If I were you," he said, clearly relishing the moment, "I'd keep a close eye on him, although that might prove difficult given how much traveling he does."

Joe turned and met Clive's icy gaze. "For your information, Mr. Damon, Blake and I are moving in together. As for what he did before we were a couple, I couldn't give a damn."

For a moment Blake wasn't sure if he had heard correctly. His heart was pounding and he stared at Joe, who was beaming at him.

"Are you serious?" he asked.

"I love you. What's a broken lease compared to that?"

They kissed passionately.

"Thanks, baby," Blake whispered. "Let's get out of here."

Blake stood and motioned for their waiter, who rushed to the table.

"Is everything all right, Mr. Danzig?"

"We're leaving," he said, handing a wad of hundred-dollar bills to the waiter. "This should cover tonight, as well as a good tip." He gestured to Clive, who was still seated. "Anything else he wants," Blake said, emboldened, "he can pay for."

The waiter took the money and walked away.

"You're making a foolish mistake," Clive said. His eyes were narrowed and he looked angrier than Blake would have ever imagined him capable.

"No, I already did that once. I'm not doing it again."

"Fine." Clive's expression was one of indifference. "I'll contact another of the shows."

"Like you said," Blake replied, "we're the best, so go ahead. Good-bye, Clive." He turned and headed toward the elevator, Joe right behind him.

Clive turned to Melody, who had remained in her seat. "What about you?" he asked. "Surely you're interested in bettering yourself."

Melody arose, terribly uncomfortable, and Hope followed her cue. "I'm happy where I am," she said, wanting to spit in the man's face. She started to go, then suddenly turned back to Clive. "And, by the way, I think you're a horrible fraud!"

❖

Back in their condo, Blake and Joe pulled and ripped at one another's clothing, desperately hungry for the naked bodies beneath.

Joe attacked Blake's hot body like an animal, biting and scratching him passionately. He pushed Blake onto the sofa and pulled off his briefs, which were already sporting a large wet spot of pre-come dripping from his erection. Joe took the boner into his mouth, hungrily deep-throating it as if he was starving. Blake groaned, the hot throat on his dick almost too much to bear. He pulled at Joe's hair, forcing him farther down onto his throbbing cock and tugging Joe's nipples. Joe suddenly stopped sucking his cock. "Wait here," he whispered, and rushed to the bedroom. He reappeared shortly, carrying condoms and lube. He unrolled a condom onto Blake's fat cock and coated it with lube. He then squatted above him and lowered himself onto the erection, slowly letting Blake fill him. Blake closed his eyes as Joe's warm body enveloped him.

"Oh, fuck, baby," he groaned. "You feel so good. Ride me."

Joe began to move rhythmically on the stiff cock, his own boner slapping against his tight stomach. "God," he gasped, "your cock fills me up."

Blake played with Joe's erect nipples as he rode his cock. Joe's ass felt so good, like it fit his dick so perfectly.

"I love you, Joe," Blake whispered.

Suddenly, as if he had said an incantation, Joe's dick sprayed come all over Blake's torso and face, even though he wasn't touching himself.

"Shit," Joe groaned, "you got me off without touching my cock."

The contractions of Joe's ass while he came were enough

to coax Blake into his own orgasm, and his body convulsed with the effort.

❖

Later, after they had showered and gotten into bed, Blake held Joe tight.

"I love you," Joe whispered also.

They kissed and Blake looked into Joe's sleepy eyes. "I will always love you," he replied, "even after you die."

CHAPTER TWENTY-TWO

Despite his initial reservations about moving into Blake's Nob Hill condominium, Joe's move went smoothly and, he had to admit, he felt at home. Though he admitted to Blake that he had always prized his Castro Street address—if only for convenience—Joe quickly fell under the spell of Nob Hill and told Blake he felt as though he had finally arrived at the place he was meant to be. And, two months later, Blake received news that his father was finally coming to San Francisco for his promised visit. Joe was understandably nervous about meeting the elder Danzig.

"What if he doesn't like me?" Joe asked. "I can always go and stay with friends while he's in town."

"Don't be crazy. My dad is great. Besides," he joked, "that's why I was smart enough to buy a two-bedroom condo."

Joe's nervousness was palpable in the days leading up to Ben's visit, however, and Blake constantly implored him to relax. "My dad knows I'm gay. Besides, why wouldn't he love you?"

Joe had no reasonable argument and so went, half-heartedly, with Blake in a rented car to the airport to pick up his father.

Even though he could easily afford a car, Blake didn't see the need for one, opting instead to walk wherever he needed to go. San Francisco, he reasoned, was one of the most walkable cities in the world and he credited this for his good physical condition. His father's visit, however, was a different thing, so he had decided to rent the car from an agency just down the hill.

They parked the rental in short-term parking, reserved for arrivals, and made their way to meet Blake's father. After a short wait, they saw Ben Danzig carrying a duffel bag and a cardboard box. Blake hugged his father and promptly took the duffel bag, over Ben's protestations.

"I can carry that," he said. "I'm not *that* old."

"How was your flight?" Blake asked, ignoring his father.

"Really nice. You didn't have to put me in first class, though."

"Dad, this is Joe, my partner."

A look of acceptance crept across Ben's face after he had appraised him and, still holding the small cardboard box, he extended his hand in greeting.

"Nice to meet you, Joe. Anyone good enough to put up with my boy is all right in my book."

Joe instantly seemed at ease with Ben and offered to carry the box, though Ben kindly refused.

"Thanks," he said, "but it's fragile and it's a gift for Blake."

As they chatted about the flight and the day in general, they walked to the parking garage in search of the rental car.

❖

When they arrived at the Nob Hill condo, Melody and her new girlfriend were waiting for them. Blake, who knew his father would like to meet his co-star, had invited them and arranged for a large spread of food to be laid out for the gathering.

"What a surprise," Ben said. He set his box down and turned to Melody. "I brought this for Blake but, what with you being a witch and all, I'll bet you'll be interested in it, too."

Everyone gathered around the table where Ben had placed the box. He opened it and carefully lifted out a large crystal ball.

"Since this was your mother's," Ben said, "I thought you'd like to have it."

Blake's eyes grew misty and he hugged his father.

"Your mother told me to bring it to you," Ben said, his face flushed.

Blake looked at his father. "What do you mean? Don't tell me you can talk to ghosts now, too."

Ben laughed nervously. "Your mother and I set up a system," he said, a twinkle in his eye. "If she wants something to go to someone, she puts their picture beside the object."

Blake regarded his father suspiciously, but it was clear from Ben's expression that he was not only telling the truth but was proud of his ingenuity.

"I wasn't sure at first," he said. "So I said 'Lila, if you want me to give this to Blake, put his picture back.' The next morning, your picture was right back in the same spot."

"Thank you," Blake whispered. "I'm not sure if I'll know how to use it."

"I'll teach you," Melody said. "I've got my own, but it's not as nice as this one."

"There's something else," Ben said, pulling two small

books from the box. "These were your mother's journals. I… we, that is, your mother and I thought you should have them, too."

Ben extracted an ornate base and placed the crystal sphere on top of it as Blake absently flipped through one of his mother's journals. They were in Spanish, and some of the earliest dates were before he had even been born. He quickly closed the book, fearing what he might find.

Suddenly, the telephone rang. Blake's first instinct was to ignore it but, at a loss for words over the gifts, he answered. It was Marty, who excitedly explained that, based on what Blake had told him about Clive's offer, the executives at FX had decided to counter with their own offer. Obviously, he explained, the big shots had viewed Clive's offer as a threat and had decided to move quickly for fear of losing their star.

"What offer?" Blake asked.

"To take the show national. No more *Haunted California*… now *Haunted America*!"

Marty continued to explain that, along with more travel, he and Melody would receive a pay increase. Blake was silent, stunned by the news.

"This is good news, kid," Marty said. "I'll come by in a couple of days with the paperwork."

"Thanks, Marty," Blake managed to say.

"Oh, and, kid," Marty said without missing a beat, "the Golden Gate Bridge thing is a go. I got the necessary permits from city hall and the studio is psyched about the idea."

"That's great." Blake was stunned by the onslaught of good news. He hung up, almost speechless. The room had fallen silent during the call and all eyes were on him. Slowly, he repeated the conversation with Marty, point by point.

"That's great news, son," Ben said. "Congratulations."

"Yeah," Blake replied unconvincingly.

"Come on." Joe threw his arms around Blake. "This is great news! I'm really proud of you, too."

Then, so no one else could hear, he whispered in Blake's ear, "We'll be fine. I'm not going anywhere."

"Thanks," Blake replied. "I really needed to hear that."

❖

After Melody and Hope left and Ben had gone off to the spare room, Blake and Joe went to bed and held each other for a long time. Eventually Joe dozed off, but Blake was unable to sleep, filled with a mixture of excitement and fear. Could they survive what was to come as a couple? Blake certainly hoped so. God knew that he loved Joe and would do anything to make things work. And the timing of the whole thing, so soon after his confrontation with Clive Damon, struck him as suspicious. Was it possible that Clive was behind it, trying to drive a wedge between him and Joe?

And then there were his mother's old journals. He wondered why his father had given them to him. He picked one up and held it in his hand. Maybe she revealed the source of his powers within the pages. He started to open it, but paused. It seemed a little invasive, he reflected, to read something so personal, something that had never been meant for someone else's eyes. He shook his head and tucked the old books away in his sock drawer. He would decide about this some other time. Right now he was tired. Tired from entertaining company, tired from the excitement of Marty's news…just tired, and all he wanted was to sleep. He would have time enough later to worry about what the future might or might not bring. Blake looked at the clock on the bedside table.

It was nearly midnight and all of San Francisco seemed quiet, save for Joe's soft snoring and the ever-present midnight whispers.

About the Author

Curtis Christopher Comer was born in Kansas but wisely fled to California when he managed to save enough money. He now lives in St. Louis with his partner, Tim, their cat, Magda, and a homicidal love bird named Raoul. When he's not writing, Curtis enjoys watching anything that deals with the paranormal and things that go bump in the night.

Curtis Christopher Comer's short stories have appeared in numerous anthologies, including *Ultimate Gay Erotica* 2005, 2006, 2007, 2008; *Best Gay Love Stories* 2005, 2006, 2007; *Dorm Porn* I and II; *My First Time, Volume Five*; *Fast Balls, Cruise Lines, Treasure Trails*, and *Starf*cker*. He co-authored the novel *Wonderland* and writes a weekly column for the *Vital Voice* in St. Louis.

Books Available From Bold Strokes Books

Whatever Gods May Be by Sophia Kell Hagin. Army sniper Jamie Gwynmorgan expects to fight hard for her country and her future. What she never expects is to find love. (978-1-60282-183-5)

nevermore by Nell Stark and Trinity Tam. In this sequel to everafter, Vampire Valentine Darrow and Were Alexa Newland confront a mysterious disease that ravages the shifter population of New York City. (978-1-60282-184-2)

Playing the Player by Lea Santos. Grace Obregon is beautiful, vulnerable, and exactly the kind of woman Madeira Pacias usually avoids, but when Madeira rescues Grace from a traffic accident, escape is impossible. (978-1-60282-185-9)

Midnight Whispers: The Blake Danzig Chronicles by Curtis Christopher Comer. Paranormal investigator Blake Danzig, star of the syndicated show Haunted California and owner of Danzig Paranormal Investigations, has been able to see and talk to the dead since he was a small boy, but when he gets too close to a psychotic spirit, all hell breaks loose. (978-1-60282-186-6)

The Long Way Home by Rachel Spangler. They say you can't go home again, but Raine St. James doesn't know why anyone would want to. When she is forced to accept a job in the town she's been publicly bashing for the last decade, she has to face down old hurts and the woman she left behind. (978-1-60282-178-1)

Water Mark by J.M. Redmann. PI Micky Knight's professional and personal lives are torn asunder by Katrina and its aftermath. She needs to solve a murder and recapture the woman she lost—while struggling to simply survive in a world gone mad. (978-1-60282-179-8)

Picture Imperfect by Lea Santos. Young love doesn't always stand the test of time, but Deanne is determined to get her marriage to childhood sweetheart Paloma back on the road to happily ever after, by way of Memory Lane-and Lover's Lane. (978-1-60282-180-4)

The Perfect Family by Kathryn Shay. A mother and her gay son stand hand in hand as the storms of change engulf their perfect family and the life they knew. (978-1-60282-181-1)

Raven Mask by Winter Pennington. Preternatural Private Investigator (and closeted werewolf) Kassandra Lyall needs to solve a murder and protect her Vampire lover Lenorre, Countess Vampire of Oklahoma—all while fending off the advances of the local werewolf alpha female. (978-1-60282-182-8)

The Devil be Damned by Ali Vali. The fourth book in the best-selling Cain Casey Devil series. (978-1-60282-159-0)

Descent by Julie Cannon. Shannon Roberts and Caroline Davis compete in the world of world-class bike racing and pretend that the fire between them is just professional rivalry, not desire. (978-1-60282-160-6)

Kiss of Noir by Clara Nipper. Nora Delany is a hard-living, sweet-talking woman who can't say no to a beautiful babe or a friend in danger—a darkly humorous homage to a bygone era of tough broads and murder in steamy New Orleans. (978-1-60282-161-3)

Under Her Skin by Lea Santos Supermodel Lilly Lujan hasn't a care in the world, except life is lonely in the spotlight—until Mexican gardener Torien Pacias sees through Lilly's facade and offers gentle understanding and friendship when Lilly most needs it. (978-1-60282-162-0)

Fierce Overture by Gun Brooke. Helena Forsythe is a hard-hitting CEO who gets what she wants by taking no prisoners when negotiating—until she meets a woman who convinces her that charm may be the way to win a battle, and a heart. (978-1-60282-156-9)

Trauma Alert by Radclyffe. Dr. Ali Torveau has no trouble saying no to romance until the day firefighter Beau Cross shows up in her ER and sets her carefully ordered world aflame. (978-1-60282-157-6)

Wolfsbane Winter by Jane Fletcher. Iron Wolf mercenary Deryn faces down demon magic and otherworldly foes with a smile, but she's defenseless when healer Alana wages war on her heart. (978-1-60282-158-3)

Little White Lie by Lea Santos. Emie Jaramillo knows relationships are for other people, and beautiful women like Gia Mendez don't belong anywhere near her boring world of academia—until Gia sets out to convince Emie she has not only brains, but beauty…and that she's the only woman Gia wants in her life. (978-1-60282-163-7)

Witch Wolf by Winter Pennington. In a world where vampires have charmed their way into modern society, where werewolves walk the streets with their beasts disguised by human skin, Investigator Kassandra Lyall has a secret of her own to protect. She's one of them. (978-1-60282-177-4)

Do Not Disturb by Carsen Taite. Ainsley Faraday, a high-powered executive, and rock music celebrity Greer Davis couldn't be less well suited for one another, and yet they soon discover passion has a way of designing its own future. (978-1-60282-153-8)

From This Moment On by PJ Trebelhorn. Devon Conway and Katherine Hunter both lost love and neither believes they will ever find it again—until the moment they meet and everything changes. (978-1-60282-154-5)

Vapor by Larkin Rose. When erotic romance writer Ashley Vaughn decides to take her research into the bedroom for a night of passion with Victoria Hadley, she discovers that fact is hotter than fiction. (978-1-60282-155-2)

Wind and Bones by Kristin Marra. Jill O'Hara, award-winning journalist, just wants to settle her deceased father's affairs and leave Prairie View, Montana, far, far behind—but an old girlfriend, a sexy sheriff, and a dangerous secret keep her down on the ranch. (978-1-60282-150-7)

Nightshade by Shea Godfrey. The story of a princess, betrothed as a political pawn, who falls for her intended husband's soldier sister, is a modern-day fairy tale to capture the heart. (978-1-60282-151-4)

Vieux Carré Voodoo by Greg Herren. Popular New Orleans detective Scotty Bradley just can't stay out of trouble—especially when an old flame turns up asking for help. (978-1-60282-152-1)

The Pleasure Set by Lisa Girolami. Laney DeGraff, a successful president of a family-owned bank on Rodeo Drive, finds her comfortable life taking a turn toward danger when Theresa Aguilar, a sleek, sexy lawyer, invites her to join an exclusive, secret group of powerful, alluring women. (978-1-60282-144-6)

A Perfect Match by Erin Dutton. The exciting world of pro golf forms the backdrop for a fast-paced, sexy romance. (978-1-60282-145-3)

Father Knows Best by Lynda Sandoval. High school juniors and best friends Lila Moreno, Meryl Morganstern, and Caressa Thibodoux plan to make the most of the summer before senior year. What they discover that amazing summer about girl power, growing up, and trusting friends and family more than prepares them to tackle that all-important senior year! (978-1-60282-147-7)

The Midnight Hunt by L.L. Raand. Medic Drake McKennan takes a chance and loses, and her life will never be the same—because when she wakes up after surviving a life-threatening illness, she is no longer human. (978-1-60282-140-8)

Long Shot by D. Jackson Leigh. Love isn't safe, which is exactly why equine veterinarian Tory Greyson wants no part of it—until Leah Montgomery and a horse that won't give up convince her otherwise. (978-1-60282-141-5)

In Medias Res by Yolanda Wallace. Sydney has forgotten her entire life, and the one woman who holds the key to her memory, and her heart, doesn't want to be found. (978-1-60282-142-2)

Awakening to Sunlight by Lindsey Stone. Neither Judith or Lizzy is looking for companionship, and certainly not love—but when their lives become entangled, they discover both. (978-1-60282-143-9)

Fever by VK Powell. Hired gun Zakaria Chambers is hired to provide a simple escort service to philanthropist Sara Ambrosini, but nothing is as simple as it seems, especially love. (978-1-60282-135-4)

Truths by Rebecca S. Buck. Two women separated by two hundred years are connected by fate and love. (978-1-60282-146-0)

High Risk by JLee Meyer. Can actress Kate Hoffman really risk all she's worked for to take a chance on love? Or is it already too late? (978-1-60282-136-1)

Missing Lynx by Kim Baldwin and Xenia Alexiou. On the trail of a notorious serial killer, Elite Operative Lynx's growing attraction to a mysterious mercenary could be her path to love—or to death. (978-1-60282-137-8)

Spanking New by Clifford Henderson. A poignant, hilarious, unforgettable look at life, love, gender, and the essence of what makes us who we are. (978-1-60282-138-5)

Magic of the Heart by C.J. Harte. CEO Susan Hettinger and wild, impulsive rock star M.J. Carson couldn't be more different if they tried—but opposites attract in ways neither woman can resist. (978-1-60282-131-6)

Ambereye by Gill McKnight. Jolie Garoul is falling in love with her assistant. The big problem is, Jolie is a werewolf. (978-1-60282-132-3)

Collision Course by C.P. Rowlands. Tragedy leaves Brie O'Malley and Jordan Carter fearful and alone. Can they find the courage to take a second chance on love? (978-1-60282-133-0)

Mephisto Aria by Justine Saracen. Opera singer Katherina Marov's destiny may be to repeat the mistakes of her father when she becomes involved in a dangerous love affair. (978-1-60282-134-7)

Battle Scars by Meghan O'Brien. Returning Iraq war veteran Ray McKenna struggles with the battle scars that can only be healed by love. (978-1-60282-129-3)

Chaps by Jove Belle. Eden Metcalf wants nothing more than to flee from her troubled past and travel the open road—until she runs into rancher Brandi Cornwell. (978-1-60282-127-9)

Lightbearer by John Caruso. Lucifer dares to question the premise of creation itself and reveals that sin may be all that stands between us and living hell. (978-1-60282-130-9)

The Seeker by Ronica Black. FBI profiler Kennedy Scott battles ghosts from her past, deadly obsession, and the evil that haunts her. (978-1-60282-128-6)

Power Play by Julie Cannon. Businesswomen Tate Monroe and Victoria Sosa are at odds in the boardroom, but not in the bedroom. (978-1-60282-125-5)

The Remarkable Journey of Miss Tranby Quirke by Elizabeth Ridley. When love enters Tranby's life in the form of a beautiful nineteen-year-old student, Lysette McDonald, she embarks on the most remarkable journey of all. (978-1-60282-126-2)

Returning Tides by Radclyffe. Insurance investigator Ashley Walker faces more than a dangerous opponent when she returns to the town, and the woman, she left behind. (978-1-60282-123-1)

Veritas by Anne Laughlin. When the hallowed halls of academia become the stage for murder, newly appointed Dean Beth Ellis's search for the truth leads her to unexpected discoveries about her own heart. (978-1-60282-124-8)

The Pleasure Planner by Larkin Rose. Pleasure purveyor Bree Hendricks treats love like a commodity until Logan Delaney makes Bree the client in her own game. (978-1-60282-121-7)

everafter by Nell Stark and Trinity Tam. Valentine Darrow is bitten by a vampire on her way to propose to her lover Alexa Newland, and their lives and love are placed in mortal jeopardy. (978-1-60282-119-4)

Beggar of Love by Lee Lynch. Jefferson is the lover every woman wants to be—or to have. A revealing saga of lesbian sexuality. (978-1-60282-122-4)